the

Small Luxury

Cookbook

SMALL LUXURY HOTELS OF THE WORLD

CONTENTS

the Small Luxury Cookbook

Published in the United Kingdom by
Ptarmigan Publishing Ltd
46 New Park Street
Devizes Wiltshire SN10 1DT

Colour origination and print:
London Print and Design plc
London & Warwick

Translation: Jacqueline Acatos

ISBN 1 904122 08 6
British Library Cataloguing in Publication Data.
A catalogue record for this book is available
from the British Library.

THE SPICE OF LIFE

Variety, they say is the spice of life, and in this book of recipes from around the world there is plenty of it. Unlike most other culinary works, it reflects no one style of cooking nor any homogenous derivation; this is a collection of signature dishes from 76 very talented chefs. What makes this book so interesting is how fresh local ingredients are used in vastly differing circumstances: from the Pacific Rim to the Great Rift Valley of Africa, Northern Europe to the Antipodes.

Until very recently that would have made this title useless as a practical cookbook. But within our lifetimes we have all been introduced to so many new and exciting things to eat: our local greengrocer or supermarket will have fresh fruit and vegetables we may never have heard of or tried before, and specialist stores are filled with spices and exotic natural products we might previously have thought were the exclusive domain of the Far East or South America. Today, new modes of transport and chill technologies mean we can enjoy a Sydney Rock Oyster almost as fresh in London as in Sydney.

The world has become a smaller place. In the pages that follow, our chefs provide both the inspiration and the means to bring the world's wealth of natural variety to your table. All masters of their profession, they have through their innovative art helped to build and establish the standard of excellence that distinguishes the Small Luxury Hotel of the World in which they work.

Bon appétit, and bon voyage.

www.slh.com

SMALL LUXURY RECIPES PAGES 6 - 43

Chicken breast stuffed with spinach and cheese

with a mushroom and tomato sauce and rösti potatoes

Serves 4

4 chicken breasts

12 fresh mushrooms, sliced

20 sun-dried tomatoes, cut into very thin strips

40g grated cheddar

2 cloves garlic, crushed

28 leaves of spinach

Nutmeg

Juice of 2 lemons

3tbs chicken stock

8tbs olive oil

Sunflower oil

Parsley for garnish

Salt & pepper

Rösti potatoes:

6 medium potatoes

100g bacon, diced

1 onion, diced

2 egg yolks

1 sprig thyme

Sunflower oil

Open the chicken breasts in the middle to make a pocket, score diagonally, and season with salt and pepper. In a pan combine half the olive oil with the garlic and spinach, adding salt, pepper and nutmeg. Once it is browned, remove it from the heat and stuff the chicken breasts first with the spinach, then the cheese.

Put the rest of the oil, the stuffed chicken fillets, the mushrooms and the tomatoes in a large saucepan. Brown the fillets on both sides, then pour over the lemon juice and add the chicken stock. Check the seasoning then cover the pan for about 10 minutes while the fillets cook and the sauce thickens.

While the fillets are cooking, scrub the potatoes and combine them with the bacon, onion, and yolks and season with salt, pepper and thyme. Separate the mixture into 12 patties, then fry in sunflower oil and drain the rösti on absorbent kitchen paper.

When the fillets are ready, cut each one into three pieces. On a plate, place three rösti potatoes at the bottom with the chicken above. Pour over the mushrooms and the sun-dried tomato sauce and garnish with the parsley.

AEGEAN SUITES HOTEL

Meggali Ammos, Skiathos, Greece

Lamb biryani

serves 4

THE OBEROI AMARVILAS, AGRA

Agra, Uttar Pradesh, India

Mix together the lamb and all the marinade ingredients, cover, and refrigerate overnight.

To prepare the rice, add the mint, coriander roots, mace, cloves, green cardamom, salt and 1tsp of ghee to approximately 2.5 litres of water. Cover the pot with a lid and boil for 45 minutes, then add the rice and cook till it is half done. Strain in a colander and spread the rice on a tray to cool.

Heat the sunflower oil in a heavy-based casserole. Add the marinated lamb and the marinade juices and braise the lamb on a low heat for approximately 10 minutes or until the marinade evaporates. Add 450ml water. Cover the pan and cook on a low heat for about 15 minutes, so that the lamb is nearly cooked but still under-done in the middle. Remove the meat and strain the gravy, keeping the solids, then return the strained gravy and the lamb to the casserole and continue cooking till the gravy reduces and the lamb is fully cooked.

The final stage of the biryani requires a pan with a heavy lid, a diameter of about 25cm and a depth of about 20cm. Line this with ghee and spread a layer of the cooked rice over the base. Spread some of the lamb and gravy on the rice, then another layer of rice on top of the meat. Sprinkle a little of the chopped mint, coriander, slit green chillies and ginger from the strained gravy over the top layer. Repeat this process until the rice and lamb is used up, but keep most of the gravy to accompany the finished biryani. The layers should reach about 3cm from the top of the pan. Tightly seal the pan with dough or aluminum foil: this ensures that no steam escapes and is essential in the cooking process (called 'dum'). Put the sealed pot into a preheated oven at 180°C and cook for around 25 minutes.

While the biryani is cooking skin, de-seed, and grate the cucumber. Whip the yoghurt till it is smooth and flowing and add the cucumber, salt, and roasted cumin powder to make the raita. Open the seal on the pan immediately before serving the biryani hot with the cucumber raita and the remaining lamb gravy.

For the marinade:

500g lamb fillet
cut into 3cm cubes,
some with the marrow bones

150g sliced onions

2 green chillies, sliced lengthwise

100g fresh mint leaves

25g ginger, thinly sliced

20g chopped fresh coriander

30g ginger garlic paste

200g whisked yoghurt

Salt to taste

50ml lemon juice

10ml rose water

3g green cardamom powder

3g clove powder

3g mace powder

2g saffron strands
soaked in 2tbs warm milk

for the rice:

700g Basmati rice

100g mint

100g coriander roots

10g whole mace

10g cloves

10g green cardamom

Salt to taste

Cucumber raita:

450g yoghurt

100g grated skinless cucumber

5g roasted cumin powder

1tsp of roasted cumin seeds

Salt to taste

125 ml sunflower oil

Ghee (or clarified butter)

Hot chocolate and Grand Marnier soufflé

with chocolate and tangerine ice cream

Serves 4

ASHDOWN PARK HOTEL

Wych Cross, East Sussex, UK

Pastry cream:

3 egg yolks

125g caster sugar

20g flour

250ml milk

25g cocoa powder

1 vanilla pod, split

100ml Grand Marnier

Ice cream:

4 egg yolks

100g sugar

125g grated chocolate

1 litre milk

Juice of 2 tangerines

Soufflé:

25g softened butter

150g caster sugar

8 egg whites

100g grated chocolate

150ml Grand Marnier

Icing sugar for coating

4 soufflé dishes,
10cm diameter and 6cm deep

Pastry cream

In a bowl, whisk the egg yolks with the sugar until pale and at the ribbon stage (extremely thick, and forms slow-to-sink ribbons on the surface when lifted). Sift in the flour and mix thoroughly.

Heat the milk, vanilla pod, and cocoa powder in a saucepan. As soon as the liquid starts to bubble pour about a third onto the egg mixture, stirring continuously. Pour the custard back into the pan and bring to the boil over a gentle heat, continuing to stir. Add the Grand Marnier, remove the vanilla pod, and pour the mixture into a shallow dish to cool quickly.

Ice cream

Reduce the tangerine juice to a syrup. Bring the milk to the boil in a pan and whisk in the grated chocolate. Whisk the egg yolks and sugar together in a bowl, then pour over the boiling milk and chocolate and return the mixture to a deep pan. Cook over a gentle heat until the mixture coats the back of a spoon. Remove from the heat and cool quickly. Add the reduced tangerine juice and churn in an ice cream machine as normal.

Soufflé

Brush the insides of the soufflé dishes with softened butter. Put 30g of sugar into one dish and rotate it so that the insides are well coated with sugar: tip the excess sugar into the next dish and repeat the process to coat them all. Pre-heat the oven to 190°C.

Warm the pastry cream in a pan and add the grated chocolate. Whisk the egg whites with the caster sugar to firm peak stage. First fold a third of the egg whites into the chocolate pastry cream, then the remainder. Pour the mixture into the dishes and smooth with a palette knife, easing the filling away from the edge of the dish with the tip of the knife. Cook on a baking tray in the oven for 18-20 minutes. To serve, arrange a ball of ice cream on the plate alongside the hot soufflé; chocolate sauce and a little candied zest complete the dish.

Blanquette of lobster

Serves 4

4 x 500g fresh lobsters
2 small carrots
1 small leek
4 shallots
50g salted butter
20ml dry white wine
10ml Noilly Prat
70ml double cream
1 packet fresh noodles or spaghetti
Salt & pepper
Freshly picked herbs

Cook the lobsters in boiling water for 12 minutes. Remove from the pan and allow to cool. Cut away the shell, keeping the head and tail (which can be washed for garnish). Slice the lobster tail in half lengthways and clean. Peel and cut the vegetables into slices about 3mm thick.

Warm the butter in a pan, soften the vegetables, then add the wine and Noilly Prat. Season and cook until the vegetables are soft. Add the cream and bring to the boil. Reduce the heat, add the lobster and simmer until the meat is hot, but do not boil.

To serve, cook, drain and season the pasta, then place it in the middle of 4 warm plates or bowls. Arrange the washed lobster shells as garnish. Taste the lobster for seasoning, add the fresh herbs, and divide onto plates. Pour the sauce and vegetables over, and serve with a side salad.

THE ATLANTIC HOTEL
St Brelade, Jersey. UK

Seared wild salmon fillet on shellfish paella

with rocket leaves and basil oil

Serves 6

6 x 150g wild salmon fillets, skinned and pin bones removed

12 fresh scallops

250g rocket

60g Parmesan shavings

Juice of half a lemon

1 bunch basil

4tbs extra virgin olive oil

Salt & freshly ground black pepper

For the shellfish paella:

180-200g mixed cooked shellfish, eg mussels, cockles and prawns

30g butter

A splash of olive oil

1 onion, finely chopped

1 garlic clove, crushed

360g paella rice (Calasparra rice)

A few saffron strands

Chicken stock (twice the volume of stock to rice, measured in a measuring jug)

2 courgettes, diced

2 red peppers, skinned, deseeded and diced

First make the basil oil. Put the basil and oil in a blender or food processor and whizz to a purée. Season to taste and set aside.

To make the paella, melt half the butter in a saucepan with the olive oil, add the onion and garlic and sweat until soft. Stir in the paella rice and cook for 3 minutes or until the rice turns translucent. Add the saffron and chicken stock, bring to the boil and simmer for 15 minutes. Stir in the courgettes and peppers and simmer for 10 minutes, until the vegetables are tender and the rice has absorbed all the liquid. Stir in the cooked shellfish, season to taste and stir in the remaining butter.

Brush the salmon fillets with olive oil and then cook in a very hot non-stick pan for 2-3 minutes on each side, until they take on a good colour. Finish with a squeeze of lemon juice. Cook the scallops in the same way. Spoon the paella into the centre of 6 serving plates, top with the salmon and arrange the scallops on either side. Dress the rocket in some of the basil oil, position on top of the salmon and scatter with the Parmesan shavings. Finally drizzle the remaining basil oil around the plate.

BALBIRNIE HOUSE

Markinch, Fife, Scotland

Baked goat cheese

with roasted pepper and endive salad

Serves 4

4 crottins of goat cheese
100ml whipping cream
1 red pepper
1 green pepper
1 yellow pepper
Salt & freshly ground black pepper

Endive salad marinade & dressing:

4 heads Belgian endive
20ml walnut oil
20ml cider vinegar
20g chopped walnuts

Bell pepper sauce:

1 red pepper
1 yellow pepper
1 large onion
Olive oil

Wash the peppers and place them whole in the oven at 200°C – no oil, butter or seasoning – and when they are brown rapidly transfer them to a plastic bag. Tightly seal and leave the peppers to steam in the bag for 10 minutes, then take them out and gently peel off their skins. Halve the peppers and remove the seeds, then cut them into strips. Marinate in the blended walnut oil, cider vinegar, and most of the chopped walnuts (keep a little back for dressing), seasoned with salt and pepper.

Cut off the bottoms of the endives and remove the leaves, which should be wiped with a clean cloth and seasoned with oil and vinegar.

Preheat the oven to 180°C. Lightly whip the cream: cut the cheeses in half, pour a little cream on the top, season with salt and pepper and place in the oven for about 10 minutes until the cheese become a little soft but still keeps its shape.

Meanwhile prepare the sauce by halving, removing the pips, and dicing the red and yellow peppers. Sauté the sliced onion and the yellow peppers in one pan and the red in another. Add a little water and simmer until the onion and the peppers are very soft. Process them separately in a blender until smooth.

Arrange the endives around the plate. Place the marinated peppers in the middle on top of the endives with the cheese above. Dust with chopped walnut and sprinkle pepper sauce around the plate. Accompany with crackers or freshly toasted baguette.

BANYAN TREE BANGKOK

Bangkok, Thailand

Smashed spiced chickpeas

Serves 6

1 x 400g tin of chickpeas, drained
(or 170g dried chickpeas, soaked and cooked until tender)

A good pinch of ground cumin seeds

1 or 2 small dried red chillies, crumbled

1 clove of garlic, peeled and pounded to a paste

Juice of 1 lemon

Salt and freshly ground black pepper

Olive oil

This is so simple: adapt the proportions of ingredients to suit your personal taste.

Smash up the chickpeas and spice them up with a good pinch of cumin. Add a little dried chilli for a touch of heat, blend in the garlic and a good squeezing of lemon juice to give it a twang, and season to taste. Finally add extra virgin olive oil for consistency and flavour.

Wok-tossed soft shell crab

with crab pomelo salad

Serves 4

Soft shell crab:

4 soft shell crabs

125g julienne of spring onion

50g julienne of green chilli

For the coating:

50g of tapioca flour

1tsp of chilli powder

Salad:

1 cooked Cornish or Tourteux crab, cleaned meat only

1tsp coriander, chopped

1tsp fresh ginger, chopped

1tsp shallots, chopped

1tsp sushi ginger, chopped

1 Thai bird chilli, chopped

1tbs Thai fish sauce

1tbs fresh lime juice

1tbs olive oil

4 leaves of iceberg lettuce, blanched

2tbs mayonnaise

1tsp wasabi paste

1tsp lime juice

Cut the crabs in half. Mix the flour with the chilli powder and a little pepper and salt, then coat and deep fry the crabs till golden brown. Transfer to a wok over a high heat and add the spring onion and the chilli: shuffle them around till the vegetables are warm but still crispy and place in the dish.

Mix all the salad ingredients and season with pepper and salt. Divide into 4 portions on the lettuce leaves and mould each into a ball by take the 4 corners of the leaf and compressing. Garnish with a coriander leaf. Mix the mayonnaise, wasabi and lime: pour the dressing into serving bowls and place the ball of salad on top.

Accompany with steamed rice.

BLAKES AMSTERDAM

Amsterdam, The Netherlands

Trilogy of New Zealand lamb:

Smoked lamb cutlet, peppered loin and rosemary sausage with minted pea purée, soused aubergine and Pinot Noir essence

Serves 6

BLANKET BAY

Glenorchy, New Zealand

4 racks of lamb
30g Manuka sawdust
1tbs cracked pepper
1tbs fresh thyme leaves
50ml olive oil

Rosemary lamb sausage:
150g short loin of lamb
1tbs fresh rosemary
Half a clove of garlic
50g chorizo sausage
50g minced pork fat
1 egg white
0.25tsp paprika

Soused aubergine:
Half an aubergine
1 clove garlic
200ml olive oil
50ml balsamic vinegar
2tbs sweet basil
2tbs Italian parsley
0.5tsp dried sumac

Pinot Noir essence:
600ml finished red wine jus
300ml Pinot Noir wine
6 sprigs fresh thyme
25g dried forest mushrooms

Pea purée:
75g mint tips
75g spinach leaves
150g baby peas
100ml light olive oil
50ml chicken stock

Garnish:
6tbs cooked white beans
6tbs tomato concassé

Trim two of the lamb racks of all bone, sinew and fat. Sprinkle on the cracked pepper, fresh thyme and olive oil. Marinade for 30 minutes. Trim the two remaining lamb racks so that the bones are very clean. Mince the lamb loin with the garlic, rosemary, chorizo and pork fat, then transfer to a food processor and blend with the egg white and cream until a smooth mousse-like consistency is achieved. Pipe out as sausages onto cling film, then wrap and tie the ends. Poach in boiling water for just 3 minutes to hold their shape, then chill. Smoke both the cleaned racks and the sausages over Manuka sawdust for five minutes, turning half way through.

Place the smoked lamb racks in a hot oven at 170°C for 7-8 minutes per lamb rack (depending on size) for medium rare. In a hot pan, brown the 2 boneless lamb loins with the sausages, then place in the oven to finish cooking (approx 5 minutes) Rest the meats well before carving. Divide the 2 smoked racks into 12 even sized cutlets. Carve the 2 boneless loins into 12 even slices. Keep warm.

Cut the aubergine into even slices, season, rub with garlic and char grill until well coloured. Pour on the measured olive oil, add the finely chopped garlic, then cook in a moderate oven (160°C) until soft. Leave to cool in the oil, then remove and dice the aubergine and return to the cooled oil, adding the fresh chopped herbs, sumac and balsamic vinegar. Leave to infuse for half an hour, then strain off the liquid. For the essence, reduce the wine with the dried mushrooms to 50ml. Add the thyme and red wine jus and bring back to the boil, then set aside for half an hour. Strain and reheat just before serving. For the purée drop the peas into boiling water and cook for three minutes. Remove from heat and add the mint tips and spinach: strain, then transfer to a food processor, add the liquids, and blend until smooth. Check and adjust the seasoning before serving.

To serve flood the plate with sauce. Spoon a mound of pea purée into the centre of the plate, place a sausage, two slices of boneless lamb loin and two smoked lamb cutlets on top. Spoon the soused aubergine neatly around, then the tomato concassé and reheated white beans. Garnish with chervil.

Fish fillet 'Veracruz'

Serves 2

1 large fish fillet, preferably sea bass

100ml extra virgin olive oil

1 onion, sliced

8 cloves garlic, chopped

3 tomatoes, skinned & seeded

250ml tomato paste

2 green peppers, sliced, skinned & deseeded

500ml chicken stock

3 bay leaves

1tsp oregano

15 green olives, pitted & halved

1tbs capers

125ml dry white wine

Sauté the onion in the olive oil for 3 minutes over a medium heat. Add the garlic and cook for 2 minutes, stirring constantly. Add the tomatoes and cook for a further 10 minutes, then the tomato paste and 5 minutes more. Add the green pepper and after 2 minutes add the chicken stock, bay leaves, oregano, olives, capers and wine. Check the seasoning and simmer for a final 5 minutes.

Heat the oven to 250°C. Put the fillet in a glass dish and cover with 250ml of the sauce, then cook in the oven for 6 minutes, turning the fillet over half way through so it cooks evenly. Serve over plantain rice and decorate with black olives.

LA CASA QUE CANTA

Guerrero, Mexico

Poached Maine lobster

with a fricassée of baby vegetables and a lobster cognac reduction

Serves 4

CASTLE ON THE HUDSON

Tarrytown, New York, USA

4 hard shell lobsters, about 800g each

5 litres court bouillon

Basil whipped potatoes:

4 medium Yukon (or other good mashing) potatoes

170ml double cream

2tbs basil oil

50g sweet butter

Salt & white pepper

For the lobster sauce:

3tbs corn oil

1tbs tomato purée

1 head fennel, thinly sliced

6 shallots, thinly sliced

1 sprig tarragon

1tsp Pernod

4tsp cognac

350ml double cream

700ml water

2 sprigs of thyme

Vegetables:

12 baby carrots

12 baby white turnips

12 baby beetroot (roasted and peeled)

20 haricot vert

Twist off the lobster claws. Bring the court bouillon to the boil and poach the claws for five minutes. Repeat with the tail meat, cooking for 7 minutes. Immerse the claws and tails in iced water and extract the meat from the shells: keep the shells for the sauce.

Peel and quarter the potatoes, boil them in salted water until tender, then process to a purée through a food mill. Fold in the warm double cream, basil oil, and butter: season to taste and keep warm.

Heat the corn oil in a 30cm pan over a high heat; when the oil is hot add the lobster shells and sear until the shells turn red. Reduce the heat and add the tomato purée, fennel, and shallots and season with salt and pepper. Cook for about 7 minutes, stirring from time to time, then add the tarragon, Pernod and cognac and cook for another minute. Stir in the cream and water, bring to the boil, and reduce for about 10 minutes. Strain through a fine sieve into small pan and set aside to keep warm.

Bring a pot of salted water to the boil and separately blanch all the vegetables except the beetroot until just tender, then refresh in an ice bath. Wrap the beetroot in foil and bake for about fifteen minutes at 170°C, when they should be tender. Remove the skins and keep them apart from the rest of the vegetables as they will bleed.

Reheat the vegetables in butter and heat the lobster meat in seasoned butter. Pipe the whipped potatoes into the centre of a large bowl or plate, surrounded by sauce. Arrange the vegetables over the sauce area; place the tail meat on the bed of potatoes and finish off with claw meat. Perfect garnished with sprigs of basil and shaved truffles.

Sea bream larded with spicy sausage

violet artichokes in 'barigoule' style, emulsion of the stock and salted butter

Serves 4

4 sea bream fillets, 180g each

50ml olive oil

12 slices chorizo

160g diced tomatoes

50g salted butter

100ml peanut oil

Chives, chopped

4 fresh basil leaves

Artichokes:

8 small violet artichokes

1 lemon

50ml olive oil

Garlic

Salt & pepper

'Barigoule' sauce:

80g shallots, finely chopped

250ml white wine

250ml chicken stock

1 sprig thyme

2 bay leaves

Remove the thick leaves, then cut the artichokes in half, rub with the lemon, and sweat in olive oil with the garlic and shallots. Add the white wine, bay leaves, thyme and stock: cover and cook gently. Skim the cooking juice off the artichokes, add the butter in small pieces to the liquid and reduce slightly.

Fry the basil leaves in peanut oil until they are crisp. Cook the tomatoes in olive oil in a pan, seasoning with salt and pepper.

Make a small pocket with a sharp knife under the skin of each fillet of sea bream. Insert three thin slices of chorizo into each pocket and fry the fish on the skin side.

Serve as shown, pouring the reduced cooking juice over the dish, adding the cut chives and decorating with the fried basil and artichoke leaves.

CHATEAU EZA

Eze Village, Côte d'Azur, France

Calf sweetbread glazed with walnut

Serves 4

800g calf sweetbreads

Peanut oil

20ml walnut oil

Butter

Sea salt

Sauce:

200ml walnut liquor

100ml calf stock, use beef if unavailable

5g fine quality walnut paste

Mushroom cakes:

160g mixed wild mushrooms

20g butter

Half a clove garlic, finely chopped

10g shallots, finely chopped

10g flour

1tbs vermouth

50ml liquid cream

20g bone marrow

20g parsley

1 egg

Vegetables:

4 radishes

4 baby leeks

2 pods broad beans

4 courgettes

100ml chicken stock

To prepare the sauce, reduce the walnut liquor by a quarter, mix in the stock and reduce the liquid to a syrup. Finish with the walnut paste and 30g of butter, then set aside to keep warm.

Clean and sauté the mushrooms with the garlic and shallots, then add the flour and cook for 5 minutes. Deglaze with the vermouth, liquid cream and the bone marrow, then leave to cool. Once cold, transfer the mushroom mixture to a blender and add the parsley and egg. Check the seasoning, then press into small moulds and cook in the oven at 170°C for 20 minutes. Remove the mushroom cakes from their moulds while still hot and keep them warm.

Meanwhile steam the vegetables and cool with cold water to fix the colours, finishing them with 70g of butter and the chicken stock. Whiten the sweetbreads with salted boiling water for 10 minutes then cool and peel.

Cook the curved side of the sweetbreads in a sauté pan with peanut oil and finish with a knob of butter, then glaze them with the sauce; the sweetbreads should be shiny when served. Place the mushroom cakes under the sweetbread, with the vegetables, sea salt and a drizzle of walnut oil around it.

HOTEL CHATEAU GRAND BARRAIL

Figeac, Saint-Émilion, France

Oriental fritters of Normandy scallops

Serves 4

12 Normandy scallops

Batter:

100g flour

330ml beer

3tbs water

2 egg whites

2tbs peanut oil

10g dehydrated seaweed

Vegetable dip:

10g celery

10g carrot

10g leek

25ml olive oil

50ml soya sauce

Caramelised tomato sauce:

50g sugar

50ml ketchup

25ml sherry vinegar

Curry sauce:

100g tomatoes, chopped

Half an onion, chopped

10ml Madras curry paste

25ml cream

For the accompaniments, heat the sugar in 100ml water until caramelised, deglaze with the vinegar and add the ketchup. For the curry sauce, fry the onions and then the tomatoes until lightly browned, then add the curry paste and cream. Bring to the boil and allow to blend. Finally, chop the vegetables into small cubes then warm them in the olive oil and soya. Allow all three to cool.

Beat the ingredients together for the light fritter batter. Remove the scallops from their shells and wash them in cold water. Dip them in the batter, ensuring that they are fully covered, then shake off any excess and deep fry for 1 minute.

Put the sauces into three small separate dishes alongside the scallops on the plate. Decorate with chive, sea salt and rocket.

CHATEAU LA CHENEVIERE

Port-en-Bessin, Huppain, France

Veal sweetbread with poached lobster tail, chickpea, almond and spice

Serves 4

2 x 500g lobsters

4 x 275g veal sweetbreads, blanched and skinned

500g pasta flour

10 egg yolks

2 eggs

Pinch of saffron strands, steeped in hot water

Mild curry spices:
- **10g turmeric**
- **2g chilli powder**
- **5g cardamom pods**
- **5g fennel seed**
- **5g coriander**
- **5g cumin seeds**

200g blanched almonds

Mirepoix vegetables (1 each carrot, onion & celery stalk, diced)

500ml fish stock

500ml whipping cream

500g chickpeas

250ml chicken stock

12 x Pak Choi leaves (or spinach)

Curry oil

Olive oil

Blanch the lobsters in boiling water for 4 minutes, then chill and shell. Separate the claws, split the tails in half and remove the entrails. Mix the pasta flour, saffron water, eggs yolk and a pinch of salt: add a splash of olive oil. Knead together, then rest for an hour before rolling out to the finest setting on a pasta machine. Cut into strips 25cm long by 5cm wide. Blanch and refresh.

Roast the curry spices in a dry pan then crush the mix. Sweat the mirepoix in hot oil, then add a pinch of the curry spice. Sweat again, add the fish stock and reduce the liquid by half. Add the cream and reduce again by half, then finely strain the curry cream.

Toast the almonds in foaming butter until they are golden brown, remove and sprinkle with salt. Cook the chickpeas in the chicken stock until they are soft, then purée and strain, keeping back a fifth for garnish. Fry the sweetbreads in foaming butter until they are golden and cooked through. Reheat the lobster in a butter and water emulsion: warm the pasta in salted water with a splash of olive oil and wrap one sheet around each sweetbread. Sit the pasta on seasoned chickpea purée in the centre of the plate. Blanch the pak choi or spinach leaves and arrange on the pasta, topped with half a lobster tail and a claw. Reheat the cooked chickpeas and almonds and scatter them around the plate. Dress with curry oil and the curry cream, foamed with a hand blender. Decorate the plate with toasted cumin and coriander seed.

THE CHESTER GROSVENOR & GROSVENOR SPA

Chester, Cheshire, UK

Fresh farm eggs with caviar and violet potato flavoured with sobrasada

Serves 4

200g violet potatoes (or other with good coloured skin)

8 fresh farm eggs

20g Sevruga caviar

40g sobrasada (a cured pork meat from Mallorca – use pancetta if unavailable)

Bay leaf

25g butter

Olive oil

Vinegar

1 bunch fresh parsley

Boil the potatoes with a bay leaf for 30 minutes, then set the pan aside to cool. Peel and drain the potato skins, then blend the potatoes and skins together in a processor with some of the liquid from the potato pan and the butter. The objective should be a creamy purée. Chop the sobrasada and warm it in a pan with a few drops of olive oil, then set aside.

To prepare the parsley oil, scald the parsley in boiling water then chill in iced water. Squeeze out the moisture and mix in a blender with a little olive oil.

Poach the eggs in swirling boiling water with some vinegar drops for 2 minutes. Arrange the potato purée in a tear shape on the plate, topped with poached eggs sprinkled with caviar. Arrange the sobrasada and parsley oil around the purée.

HOTEL CLARIS

Barcelona, Spain

Chicken '59 Knives'

Serves 4

4 x 220g chicken fillets

12 lollo (Chinese lettuce) leaves

4 cherry tomatoes

200ml dry white wine

4tbs natural yoghurt

200ml double cream

Butter mixture;

400g unsalted butter

80g crushed garlic

120g spring onions, finely chopped

40g coriander, finely chopped

40g cumin

40g mixed spices

32g crushed pepper corns

10g marjoram

20g salt & pepper

Vegetables:

2 carrots

2 courgettes

4 stalks asparagus

Prepare the butter mixture for the sauce a few hours in advance as it needs to be frozen. Melt the butter and mix in all the other ingredients. Allow the mixture to cool but not solidify, then pour it out across the width of a rectangle of cling film and roll into a cylinder shape. Leave the wrapped 'butter sausage' in the freezer to become solid before using.

Remove the cling film and melt the frozen butter mixture in a pan. Cut the chicken into thick strips and sauté them in the butter, then add the wine. Leave to cook until all the wine is absorbed. Add the yoghurt, using a wooden spoon to ensure it is fully combined around the bottom of the pan, then stir the cream into the other ingredients in the pan. Leave the pan to simmer.

Wash and clean the carrots and courgettes, cut them into 'julienne' matchsticks and parboil them in boiling salted water. Cut the asparagus stalks in half and par boil these as well: it is important that the vegetables should not be overcooked. Serve with rice and garnished with lollo leaves and cherry tomatoes as shown.

THE CLASSIC HOTEL

Nicosia, Cyprus

Seared sesame crusted tuna steak

with wilted spinach, bean sprouts, confit potatoes, and bell peppers; served with pesto oil and glazed cherry tomatoes

Serves 2

I x 200g tuna loin steak shaped into a cylinder

50ml olive oil

I small red onion, finely diced

I clove garlic, finely chopped

50g spinach leaves

25g Mung bean sprouts

I red pepper skin removed, deseeded and thinly sliced

I yellow pepper skin removed, deseeded and thinly sliced

Juice of I lemon

3 cherry tomatoes, halved

50g mixed black & white sesame seeds

I egg white (beaten)

Salt & pepper

Confit potatoes:

150g duck fat

100g new potatoes

2 cloves garlic, peeled

2 sprigs of fresh thyme

Pesto oil:

75ml extra virgin olive oil

I clove garlic

50g fresh basil leaves

50g grated Parmesan

25g toasted pine nuts

Plantain crisp:

I plantain, peeled and thinly sliced lengthways

Fry in very hot oil until golden brown

To prepare the pesto oil coarsely chop the basil and garlic and transfer to a food processor. Add half the olive oil, Parmesan and pine nuts and pulse until the pesto reaches a rough consistency. Mix the remainder of the olive oil slowly and season to taste with salt and pepper. Put aside until ready to use.

For the confit potatoes, cut the potatoes into a dice, then wash and pat the cubes dry with a kitchen towel. Bring the duck fat to the boil, then add the garlic and thyme. Reduce the heat to a simmer and add the potatoes. Cook until tender, then remove from the fat and drain.

Preheat a medium sauté pan with 25ml of olive oil, then add the onion and garlic, shaking the pan occasionally, until they are soft but without colour. Add the spinach, bean sprouts, peppers and tomatoes. Cook for 4-5 minutes stirring consistently: check and adjust the seasoning.

Season the tuna loin with salt, pepper and lemon juice. Lightly brush with the beaten egg white and roll in the sesame seed mix until the fish is well coated. Heat the remainder of the olive oil in a casserole pan: when it is very hot add the tuna loin and sear on all sides for about 3-4 minutes – it should be pink inside and golden brown on the outside. Remove from the pan.

Toss the sautéed spinach mixture with the confit potatoes and arrange them in the centre of the plate. Cut the tuna on the angle and position on top of the spinach mixture. Drizzle pesto oil around and garnish with cherry tomatoes and plantain crisps.

CORAL REEF CLUB

St James, Barbados, West Indies

Stuffed Jamaican Jerk chicken breast

with sautéed calaloo, mango salsa and braised black beans

Serves 4

4 chicken breasts, butterflied and pounded flat

1 large ripe plantain cut in 4 lengthways

4 strips roasted pimento pepper

200g calaloo or spinach leaves, blanched

Half a cup black beans (soaked overnight)

100g smoked bacon, chopped (pimento smoked if available)

25g onion, chopped

2 cloves garlic, finely chopped

10ml lager beer (Red Stripe recommended)

8 baby carrots

1 tablespoon honey

1 fresh corn on the cob

1 green banana

60ml vegetable oil

60ml olive oil

Salt & pepper

Immerse the chicken breasts in the jerk marinade for a couple of hours, then take out the meat. Heat the oven to 180°C. Wrap the plantain and roast pepper strips in a few of the calaloo (or spinach) leaves, then roll these up tightly inside the chicken breasts. Bake in the oven for about 15 minutes until the chicken is cooked. Meanwhile set the black beans to simmer and drain them when tender. Sauté the bacon, half the onion and one clove of garlic, then add the beans and the beer and simmer until most of the beer has evaporated. Check and adjust the seasoning. Boil the carrots until tender, then glaze with the honey in a sauté pan.

Sauté the rest of the onion and garlic and add the remaining calaloo leaves, stirring gently for 3 to 4 minutes until they are cooked. Rub the corn with olive oil and salt and cook under a hot grill or on a hot skillet to roast and caramelise the kernels, then remove the kernels from the cob. Slice the green banana thinly lengthways and fry until crisp in hot vegetable oil: season.

To serve, slice the stuffed chicken breasts at an angle. Centre the black beans on the plate and place one piece of chicken standing upright with a couple of slices alongside. Make a 'nest' shape with the sautéd calaloo and fill it with roasted corn kernels. Garnish with green banana chips, mango salsa, glazed carrots and fresh herbs.

COYABA BEACH RESORT & CLUB

Montego Bay, Jamaica, West Indies

Jerk marinade:
combine all ingredients and blend

1 spring onion, chopped

2 cloves garlic, minced

Half a Scotch Bonnet (or Habanero) pepper, chopped fine

1 teaspoon ground pimento (allspice)

0.5tsp ground fresh nutmeg

0.5tsp ground black pepper

0.5tsp paprika

4tbs olive oil

1tsp fresh thyme

2tbs soy sauce

Salt to taste

Mango salsa:
combine all ingredients

1 large ripe mango

25g red onion, diced

1tsp fresh ginger, chopped fine

0.5tsp garlic, minced

1tsp fresh chopped cilantro

2tbs fresh lime juice

1tbs virgin olive oil

1tbs balsamic vinegar

0.25tsp chilli pepper, chopped fine

Salt & pepper to taste

SMALL LUXURY RECIPES PAGES 46 - 83

Roast Anjou pigeon with vinegar jus

Serves 4

DANESFIELD HOUSE HOTEL & SPA

Marlow-on-Thames, Buckinghamshire, UK

4 Anjou pigeons, cleaned and trussed

Honey pickled shallots:

12 shallots

250ml honey

1litre water

250ml white wine vinegar

Vegetables:

125g girolles cleaned

2 little gem lettuce, shredded

10g butter

Sea salt & pepper

Vinegar sauce:

Wings and necks of the pigeon, chopped finely

4 shallots, finely diced

1 clove garlic, crushed

2 sprigs thyme

1/8 bay leaf

200ml white wine vinegar

100ml dry white wine

600ml fresh chicken stock

5g butter to finish

Sea salt & pepper

Pommes au lard:

450g dry weight potatoes

125g shallots diced

1 clove garlic, crushed

125g Alsace bacon, diced

25g butter

Sea salt & pepper

4 x 6cm metal rings

Both the honey pickled shallots and vinegar sauce can be made up to 4 days before. For the former, peel the shallots, place in a pan with all the ingredients and simmer for 20-30 minutes. When done, leave to cool in the liquor. For the sauce, sear the pigeon trimmings in a hot heavy bottomed saucepan until golden brown, then add the shallots, garlic and herbs and cook until soft. Add the vinegar and wine and reduce dry, then add the chicken stock and reduce to 200ml. Pass through a fine sieve and leave to cool.

The pommes au lard can be prepared a day in advance: cook the onions and garlic in the butter until soft and translucent, add the bacon and cook for a further 5 minutes, then leave to cool. Boil the peeled potatoes, then press through a ricer. Blend the cooled onion and bacon with the potatoes, add seasoning to taste and place the mix into the buttered rings, levelling out until it reaches the top of the ring.

In a hot pan sauté the girolles in the butter for about 2 minutes, season, add the shredded lettuce, then take the pan off the heat and allow the leaves to finish cooking in the residual heat.

Preheat the oven to 200° C. Season the pigeons inside and out, then seal in a hot pan and roast for 10 minutes, then leave somewhere warm for 5-10 minutes to rest. Colour the potatoes on one side in butter, transfer to the oven for 15 minutes, keep warm.

Peel the outside skin from the pickled shallots and sauté in butter until hot, then add the girolles and lettuce. Check and adjust the seasoning. Deglaze the roasting pan with the vinegar sauce, whisk in the 5g of butter, check the seasoning, and serve as shown.

Baked lobster

with green beans, herb vinaigrette and tomato sorbet

Serves 4

2 x 600g lobsters

2tbs olive oil

Sea salt

Paprika

100g green beans

For the sorbet:

4 tomatoes

1 heaped tsp sea salt

1 heaped tsp black pepper

Basil

100ml sugared water

2 soup spoons tomato ketchup

2 soup spoons tomato purée

For the vinaigrette: combine all ingredients

0.5tsp each;

- **Basil**
- **Chervil**
- **Parsley**
- **Spinach**
- **Cilantro**

3tsp extra virgin olive oil

1tsp white wine vinegar

Juice of 1 lemon

Blend the tomatoes with the rest of the sorbet ingredients. Pass the liquid through a fine sieve and whisk to a light sorbet consistency. Freeze until required, then scoop into a small pot for each serving.

Prepare the lobsters by cutting them in half and removing the entrails. Break the claws, and fry the meat in olive oil, adding a sprinkle of paprika and sea salt. Cook for 2 minutes and keep warm. Lightly boil the beans and keep them warm in their cooking liquid.

Dress the lobster and arrange with the beans on top and surrounded by the vinaigrette. Garnish the tomato sorbet with herbs.

DIE SWAENE

Bruges, Belgium

Seared sea scallops

caramelised pineapple and Alsace bacon

Serves 4

8 large diver scallops

Juice of half a lemon

200g Alsace bacon (or Pancetta)

2 sheets baking paper

2 heads frisée lettuce

50ml olive oil

Sprig of chervil

For the caramel:

1 sweet pineapple

250ml water

200g sugar

200ml white wine vinegar

For the purée:

1 head celeriac

300ml milk

250ml water

20g cold butter

Open and clean the scallops, taking care not to tear the meat. Slice each one into 3 pieces and leave out on a dry cloth.

Slice the bacon into strips about 2mm wide by 12cm long. Place the strips between sheets of baking paper on a baking tray, then weigh down the paper with another baking tray to prevent the bacon curling. Bake for approximately 10 minutes at 170°C until crisp, then allow to cool.

Cut off and discard the dark green leaves from the frisée. Separate the white from the yellow, keeping only the yellow. Wash and dry the leaves.

Peel and dice the pineapple into 2mm cubes. To make the caramel, boil the sugar and water in a heavy based pan until the liquid is golden in colour. Add the pineapple dice and the white wine vinegar: the latter will stop the caramel from cooking and add acidity. Allow to cool.

Cut the celeriac into a large dice and bring to the boil in the milk and water. Allow to simmer for 10 minutes: when just cooked, strain the celeriac, keeping back the liquor. Purée the celeriac with the butter, adding liquor until the desired consistency is reached (the purée should be just dropping off a spoon). Season and keep warm.

Fry the scallops until golden in nonstick pan. Turn for a few seconds, adding the lemon juice. Do not overcook!

To serve, make 5 dots of the purée around the outside of the plate with pineapple between each. Dress the frisée with olive oil, season, and arrange in the middle of the plate topped with 2 strips of bacon. Place 1 scallop piece on each dot of purée, drizzle caramel around and garnish with chervil.

DORSET SQUARE HOTEL

London, England

Tournedos of veal

with aubergine, courgette and Pligouri in a tomato and basil sauce

Serves 4

EAGLES PALACE

Halkidiki, Greece

Begin a day in advance by slicing the leek lengthwise, then selecting and lightly boiling 4 of the strips. These will later be used to bind the tournedos. Chop the rest of the leek, combine with the wine, chopped basil, oil, salt and black pepper, and marinate the veal fillets in the mixture overnight.

The next day, wash and slice the aubergines lengthwise to a thickness of about 3mm. Wash and slice the courgettes the same way. Cook both vegetables in oil until soft, then lay out the slices on kitchen paper to absorb the oil.

For the Pligouri, sweat the onion in the oil then add the bulgur wheat and chicken stock. Check and adjust the seasoning, then simmer for twenty minutes. Remove from the heat and add the butter, then leave with the lid on to allow the wheat kernels to expand.

Sweat the onion and garlic for the sauce in the oil, then add the tomatoes. After a couple of minutes add the beef stock, check the seasoning, and simmer for fifteen minutes. Finally add the butter, cheese, and a little chopped basil to taste.

When ready to serve, season the marinated tournedos with salt and pepper, then bind slices of aubergine and courgette to them with the strips of leek. Carefully sauté both sides of the fillets in the oil until browned, then add the sauce and cook the meat and the vegetables together for a few minutes before serving.

To serve, place a 10cm ring in the middle of the plate. Half fill the ring with Pligouri, then top with a veal tournedos. Remove the ring and pour over the sauce: decorate with grated Feta cheese and fresh basil.

4 veal tenderloin fillets, 180g each

320g aubergines

320g courgettes

1 leek

80ml white wine

Basil

Olive oil

Salt & black pepper

For the Pligouri
(a traditional Greek cereal dish):

20ml olive oil

80g onion, chopped

160g bulgur wheat

320ml chicken stock

20g butter

Salt & white pepper

For the sauce:

40ml olive oil

80g onion, chopped

4 cloves garlic, chopped

400g chopped tomatoes

200ml strong beef stock

20g butter

40g Feta cheese

Fresh basil

Salt & black pepper

Venison steak

with pancetta-wrapped Te Pania Paua,
braised fennel bulb and Moi Moi potatoes

Serves 4

4 x 180g venison steaks, Denver leg recommended

8 x Te Pania Paua (or other meaty shellfish)

4 x fennel bulb

12 x Moi Moi (or other fragrant) potatoes

500ml white wine

8 slices pancetta

100g butter

4 cloves garlic

1 onion

Trim the sinew from the venison leg and cut four 180g steaks. Hold the paua in the hand and slide the blade of an oyster knife into the muscle, keeping the blade as close to the shell as possible. Extract the paua and, on a cutting board, remove the hard radula at the foot of the flesh. Wash and place on a dry cloth, tightly wrap the paua in pancetta, put a knob of butter in the shell and replace the wrapped paua on top.

Wash and cut the fennel bulbs into quarters and remove the core. Wash and peel the potatoes and place them with the garlic, onion, and fennel in a braising dish. Cover with the white wine and braise until soft – about 40 minutes. Transfer the liquid to another pan and reduce by two thirds.

Put the seasoned venison in a hot pan with the paua and roast for 8 minutes at 220°C. Once cooked, deglaze the pan with the reduced braising liquid and add a knob of butter. Place the reheated moi moi and fennel on a plate, slice the venison, and arrange the paua. Pour sauce over the top and around the dish.

EICHARDT'S PRIVATE HOTEL
Queenstown, New Zealand

Fillet of venison (Eland) with duo pepper sauce

Serves 4

EKLAND SAFARIS

South Africa

4 x 250g venison fillet medallions

2 cloves garlic crushed

10 ml dried thyme

Olive oil

For the sauce:

4tbs olive oil

1 medium onion, finely chopped

3tbs crushed black peppercorns

2tbs green peppercorns Madagascar

0.5tsp ground cloves

3 cloves of garlic, peeled and finely chopped

30ml brandy

2tbs beef stock powder

500ml water

125ml double cream

Vegetables:

1 each green, yellow and red pepper, roasted, peeled and sliced with a dash of olive oil

1 large bunch spinach, coarsely chopped

250g cherry tomatoes

10ml salt

125ml olive oil

Rub the thyme, garlic and a little olive oil into the meat and allow it to sit for at least 30 minutes.

For the sauce, sauté the onions in olive oil until transparent. Add the crushed black pepper, green peppercorns, cloves and garlic. Keep stirring, adding the beef stock powder once all the ingredients are blended. Add the brandy, then little by little the water, then simmer for another 3 minutes while the sauce thickens. Add the cream and keep warm: if it is too thick, thin the sauce with water.

Heat a large non-stick frying or griddle pan. Season the steaks on both sides with salt and pepper and sear for approximately 2 minutes on each side: feel free to cook for more or less time, to your liking. Leave the meat to rest while you prepare the vegetables.

Bring a large pan half filled with salted water to the boil. Add the spinach and cook uncovered for 2 minutes, then strain. Heat the olive oil in the same pan and saute the cherry tomatoes for 30 seconds, then toss in the spinach and stir fry for 1 minute.

To serve form a bed of spinach and tomatoes, place the steak on top, pour sauce over the dish, and top with roasted peppers and a sprinkling of fresh thyme.

Pan seared sea bass

with a ragoût of fingerling potatoes, roasted fennel, exotic mushrooms and spinach saffron sauce

Serves 4

To prepare the saffron sauce, warm a tablespoon of olive oil in a medium pan, add the mushroom trimmings, shallots, garlic and saffron, and sweat for 2-3 minutes. Add the cracked pepper, bay leaf and vermouth. Reduce the vermouth by three quarters and add the cream, then simmer for about 5 minutes or until the sauce becomes thick enough to coat the back of a spoon. Remove from the heat, finish with a tablespoon of butter and season with salt and pepper. Strain through a fine sieve and set aside.

Heat the oven to 190°C. Halve the fingerling potatoes lengthways and, on a baking tray, season them with a tablespoon of olive oil, salt and pepper. Bake for about 12 minutes until they are a good golden brown and cooked through. Meanwhile remove the stalks and slice the fennel bulb into matchsticks, then coat with same seasoning as the potatoes and bake on a tray for 8 minutes. Take the vegetables out of the oven and set aside.

Heat 2 tablespoons of olive oil with a tablespoon of butter in a sauté pan and cook the mushrooms until slightly soft. Add the fingerling potatoes, fennel and spinach. Continue cooking until the spinach is wilted and the mushrooms are tender. Season with salt, pepper and chopped herbs. Set aside and keep warm.

Heat the oven to 200°C. Season the sea bass fillets with salt and pepper and dust them in the flour. Heat 2 tablespoons of olive oil in an oven proof pan; when the oil is very hot sear the fillets on one side for about 2 minutes, then turn them over and cook in the oven for 5-7 minutes until they are firm to the touch. Meanwhile, warm a tablespoon of olive oil and a tablespoon of butter in a small sauté pan and add the tomatoes and blanched carrots, cooking until they are heated through. Finish with salt, pepper and chopped herbs.

To serve, spread a quarter of the saffron sauce over each plate. Divide the ragoût into the centre of each plate; put the sea bass on top and garnish with carrots, tomatoes and micro greens.

4 x 175-200g sea bass fillets

8 fingerling potatoes

1 bulb of fresh fennel

250g exotic mushrooms (eg shiitake, oyster & portobella) sliced or roughly chopped

150g baby spinach

3tbs trimmings from the exotic mushrooms

3tbs chopped shallots

0.5tsp chopped garlic

1bay leaf

0.25tsp cracked pepper

1tsp saffron threads

325ml dry vermouth

500ml double cream

4 baby carrots, cut in half and blanched

8 cherry tomatoes

2tbs chopped mixed herbs (basil, chervil, chives & parsley)

2tbs flour

Butter

Olive oil

Salt & white pepper

Micro greens for garnish

ENCHANTMENT RESORT

Sedona, Arizona, USA

Pan seared striped marlin

with kumara & ginger dauphinoise, poached oysters, baby vegetables and tomato consommé

Serves 4

4 x 140g marlin medallions

2tbs powdered scallop roe

12 oysters,
Clevedon Coast if available

12 baby carrots, peeled

Chervil

Chives

Coriander

Kumara & ginger dauphinoise:

500g peeled golden kumara (sweet potato)

200ml double cream

25g sliced ginger root

Tomato consommé:

2 sticks lemon grass

4 large tomatoes

1 bird's eye chilli

2 shallots

2 cloves garlic

15g ginger

2tbs chopped coriander

6 lime leaves

4 coriander seeds

1tbs fish sauce

150ml fresh tomato juice

1 litre fish or chicken stock

Bash the lemongrass and chop all the other solid ingredients for the consommé. Bring all the ingredients to the boil in a large pan, then allow to simmer gently for half an hour. Purée the liquid in a large blender to release all the flavour, then pass through a strainer and allow to cool. Clarify as you would for a consommé.

Gently warm the cream and ginger together with a little salt and pepper. Meanwhile, slice the kumera on a mandolin to 1mm thick and spread out a layer of the slices in a buttered dish at least 4cm deep. Brush the layer with the cream mixture and repeat until the dish is full to the top. (Depending on the size of the dish you may need more kumara than indicated: bear this in mind when selecting your dish.) Cover with tin foil and bake at 160°C until the dauphinoise is soft in the centre: subject to the size of dish this will take about 45 minutes. Allow the contents to cool, then turn out of the dish and cut into rounds with a cookie cutter.

Heat the oven to 200°C. Roll the marlin in the powdered scallop roe seasoned with salt and pepper, then transfer the coated fish to the warming drawer to gently gain in temperature. When it is warm to the touch pan fry until golden on both sides and bake in the oven for 3-4 minutes.

When ready to assemble the dish, warm through the kumara dauphinoise in a moderate oven. Heat up two thirds of the consommé: cook the carrots in a pot of salted boiling water until al dente, bring the remaining consommé to just below boiling and lightly poach the oysters (about 3 minutes) in the liquid. Make up four herb salads from the leaves and dress them with a little olive oil and lemon juice. Serve as shown in a warmed bowl plate.

Grilled Providenciales lobster tail

Serves 4

4 medium lobster tails: about 400g each

100ml olive oil

For the rice:

300g basmati rice

1 medium carrot

1 medium broccoli head, chopped

20g fresh peas

50g shredded coconut

1 medium tomato, peeled and deseeded

For the lobster butter:

2 carrots, diced

1 medium onion, thinly sliced

2 cloves garlic, thinly sliced

Half a leek, diced

5 medium tomatoes, peeled and deseeded

1 sprig fresh thyme

1 bay leaf

20ml white wine

500 gram unsalted butter

2 sprigs fresh basil

Soak the rice for 1 hour in cold water. Peel and dice the carrot and clean the broccoli.

Cut the lobster tails in half and take out and store the flesh in the fridge. Heat the oil in a medium saucepan, and when it is very hot insert the lobster shells. When they start to turn red add the carrots, onion, garlic, leek, tomatoes, thyme and bay leaf. Cook for two minutes, then deglaze the pan with the wine. Add the butter and basil and cook at medium heat until the butter is clarified. Strain the liquid and leave at room temperature.

Strain the rice and cook in boiling water. While it is cooking blanch the carrot, peas and broccoli. When the rice is cooked mix in the carrot, peas and shredded coconut.

Grill the lobster tails. Be sure not to overcook: the best way to serve them is medium to medium rare. Arrange the rice in the middle of the plate topped with lobster meat. Decorate with broccoli around the lobster and rice. Serve the lobster butter on the side.

GRACE BAY CLUB

Providenciales, Turks & Caicos Islands

Gratinated lemon and lime mousse

with bitter orange sauce and lime syrup

Serves 4

35ml lemon juice

35ml lime juice

60ml double cream

25g sugar

10g cornflour

65g egg yolk

5g gelatine leaves (2)

Green food colouring

Italian meringue:

240g sugar

22g egg white

80ml water

25g glucose

Icing sugar

Bitter orange sauce:

400ml fresh orange juice

75g sugar

200g butter

Orange liqueur (Grand Marnier) to taste

Soak the gelatine leaves in cold water. Meanwhile, bring the lemon and lime juice to the boil with the double cream. Beat the egg yolks with sugar and add the cornflour, then pour the hot cream, lemon and lime over the egg mixture. Blend, return the combined mixture to the saucepan and bring back almost to the boil, then add the gelatine to the hot mixture and remove from the heat.

Make the Italian meringue by heating the water and sugar to 118°C (between soft ball and hard ball). Meanwhile, whisk the egg whites to snow, then pour the hot sugar syrup into the egg whites, whisking all the time. Beat until cold.

Fold the meringue into the lemon and lime mixture. Set out four open circular moulds (10cm diameter) on cling film: spoon the lemon and lime mixture into the moulds, flattening the tops, and freeze for at least 3 hours. Release the moulds by running a hot knife around the edges. Sprinkle generously with icing sugar and caramelise with a blowtorch. Do not use the grill as the heat is not intense enough.

To make the bitter orange sauce, heat the sugar in a pan until it caramelises then add the orange juice. Reduce the liquid by half until it is syrupy, then thicken it by adding the cold butter in lumps. Add a dash of orange liqueur to taste.

To make the lime syrup, zest the lime with a peeler, ensuring there is no pith, and finely cut the peel into a julienne. Cook in a little very heavily sugared water for two minutes, then add a drop of green food colouring and leave to cool.

THE GRAND HOTEL

Eastbourne, Easts Sussex, UK

Lamb cutlets

flavoured with rosemary, potato basket with vegetables in aniseed butter

Serves 4

1.2kg lamb cutlets

2 sprigs each rosemary & thyme

4 cloves garlic

Extra virgin olive oil

300g baby carrots

300g green asparagus

8 spring onions

4 potatoes

10g aniseed

80g butter

Salt & pepper

Lamb sauce (makes 200g):

1kg lamb bones

100g onions, chopped

100g each carrots, celery and leeks, chopped

5 cloves of garlic

1 sprig each thyme & rosemary

2tbs tomato pulp or concentrate

50g butter

Olive oil

200ml red wine

1 litre water

Bay leaf

Pepper

Marinade the cutlets in an infusion of the rosemary, thyme, chopped garlic and extra virgin olive oil for about 2 hours.

Cut the lamb bones into small pieces and brown them in a pan with a little olive oil. Add the diced vegetables, the tomato pulp and wine: mix well and cook for a few minutes more. Pour the water over the mixture and add the rosemary, part of the thyme, garlic and a little pepper. Leave to cook over a low heat for 1 hour, degreasing and skimming the surface regularly. Strain, return to the pot and reduce the stock to half. Add the rest of the thyme leaves, butter, salt and pepper. Keep hot until the dish is ready to serve.

Thoroughly wash and peel the carrots, asparagus and spring onions; slice the carrots lengthwise. Steam all the vegetables.

Using a spiral cutter prepare thin strips of potatoes and wrap them around four 2-3cm high steel cylinders of various diameters. Deep fry for a few minutes in olive oil to fix the potato shapes: repeat the operation 4 times, in order to get 4 basket arrangements per serving. Drain the potato cylinders on kitchen paper, slide the rings off and keep them hot.

Meanwhile glaze all the vegetables with butter and aniseed in another frying pan. Season with salt and pepper. Keep hot.

Remove the cutlets from the marinade, add salt and pepper and cook them in another frying pan using the remaining butter, thyme and garlic. Keep hot.

Compose the baskets directly on the plate by linking together the 4 potato rings as shown: stuff with the carrots, asparagus and spring onions. Place the lamb cutlets in the middle, pour the sauce around and garnish with small sprigs of rosemary.

GRAND HOTEL MAJESTIC

Pallanza, Italy

Rhubarb pancake with strawberry ice cream parfait, blackcurrant sorbet and passion fruit sauce

Serves 4

GRAND HOTEL VILLA CASTAGNOLA

Lugano, Switzerland

Stewed rubarb

Cut the rhubarb into matchsticks and spread these over a baking tin, then add the white wine, sugar and pomegranate syrup. Leave to marinate for 1 hour, then cook in the oven at 150°C for 30 minutes.

Stewed rhubarb:

200g fresh peeled rhubarb

100ml white wine

50g sugar

50g pomegranate syrup

Ice cream parfait

Whisk the caster sugar with the egg yolk until it is a soft mousse, then add the fresh strawberry pulp. Whip the cream and fold it into the mixture, then pour the parfait into moulds and place in the freezer to set.

Ice cream parfait:

40g caster sugar

1 egg yolk

50g fresh strawberry pulp

100ml whipping cream

Blackcurrant sorbet

Bring the water, sugar and glucose to the boil. Remove from the heat and add the pulp, then process in a sorbet machine or freeze, forking occasionally to prevent setting solid.

Blackcurrant sorbet:

100g blackcurrant pulp

50ml water

30g sugar

1tsp glucose

Passion fruit sauce

Take out the pulp from the passion fruit, add the sugar and cook gently for 30 minutes. Use the sauce to decorate the plates when finishing the dessert preparation.

Passion fruit sauce:

5 passion fruit

50g sugar

Quark pancake

For the pancake batter mix together the flour, milk, cheese, and egg yolk. Whisk the egg white with the sugar and blend into the rest of the ingredients. Use a piping bag to prepare round cakes for cooking in an appropriate pan.

Take the pancake out of the pan, spread it with the stewed rhubarb, roll the pancake and cut into two. Put one piece on each dish and decorate with fresh strawberries and mint leaves.

Quark pancake:

50g flour

80ml milk

150g Quark (a soft, unripened cottage cheese)

1 egg yolk

1 egg white

40g caster sugar

Fillet of veal

in a mille-feuille of crispy potatoes with a Montalcino red wine sauce

Serves 4

4 x 130g fillets of veal

4 potatoes

60g shallots

500ml red Montalcino wine

100ml brown gravy

600g mixed seasonal vegetables

Extra virgin olive oil

Salt & pepper

Aromatic herbs for garnish: chervil, chives, parsley, tarragon

Peel and cut the potatoes into discs 1cm thick: bring to the boil in salted water then immerse immediately in iced water. Repeat with the vegetables. Fry the shallots in a pan with just a little oil and then add the wine. When the sauce has reduced to a third, incorporate the brown gravy and cook for a further 10 minutes. Leave the sauce to keep warm.

Fry the fillets in oil with a little salt and pepper until lightly browned. Reheat the potatoes and vegetables. Place a fillet in the centre of each plate between the potatoes and place the vegetables next to it. Finish off with the sauce and aromatic herbs.

GROTTA GIUSTI SPA HOTEL

Monsummano Terme, Tuscany, Italy

Lemon chilli sea bass

Serves 6

6 x 175g loins of sea bass

500g green tomatoes

75g serrano chillies

100g onions

25g cilantro (chopped fresh coriander leaves)

100ml lemon juice

1kg potatoes

150g butter

150g Parmesan

300ml crème fraîche

Prepare the sauce by mixing the green tomato, chillies, onion, cilantro, and lemon juice in a blender: season with salt. To make the potato purée boil the peeled potatoes, pass them through a sieve and mix with the butter, crème fraiche and Parmesan.

Grill the loins until they are cooked on both sides, then serve on a bed of potato purée topped with the green tomato sauce.

Garnish with chopped red onion and a bouquet of fresh chives.

HOTEL HABITA

Col. Polanco, Mexico

Pyramid of shrimp on a bed of mango rice

Serves 4

24 medium size shrimp, shelled and deveined

12 cherry tomatoes

12 large green onions (or 12 quarters of medium white onion)

1 package bamboo sticks, 12cm long

2 limes

6 sprigs of fresh rosemary

Optional:

Basil leaves and mango for decoration

Roasted green chilli strips

For the mango rice:

250g long grain white rice

2tbs olive oil

375ml chicken stock

125ml fresh orange juice

2 mangos, peeled and cut into 1cm pieces

2 green chillies, freshly roasted, peeled and diced (or 1 x 100g can of diced green chillies, drained)

For the marinade:

50ml white vinegar

4tbs rice vinegar

1tbs sesame oil

3tbs soy sauce

0.5tbs oregano

1tsp paprika

1tbs ginger, minced

1.5tsp salt

Half a jalapeño chilli, finely chopped

1.5tbs garlic, finely chopped

2tbs parsley, finely chopped

2 whole green onions, finely sliced

Mix together all the ingredients for the marinade. Transfer with the shrimps to a plastic zip lock bag or other sealed container and marinate for 2 hours or overnight in the refrigerator.

Soak the bamboo sticks in cold water for 30 minutes. Wash and drain the rice, and let it sit for 15 minutes in a colander. Heat the olive oil in a pan over a medium high heat and sauté the rice for 3 minutes or until very lightly browned. In another pan bring the chicken stock and orange juice to the boil, then add the rice, mango and green chilli. Cook for approximately 15 minutes covered on a medium heat.

Meanwhile, assemble the brochettes on the bamboo sticks. Skewer a piece of shrimp, a cherry tomato, an onion (or piece) and another shrimp to finish. Cook on a hot grill for about 3 minutes on each side.

Plate the dish with rice in the center, moulding the rice firmly within a metal measuring cup. For each plate secure 3 of the grilled shrimp brochettes pyramid style with half a lime at the top. For extra height and presentation top the lime with a sprig of rosemary. As a further optional decoration, cut three small pieces of mango with a heart shaped cutter to anchor each brochette: shown here with a few fresh basil leaves and extra strips of freshly roasted green chilli.

HACIENDA DE LOS SANTOS

Alamos, Sonora, Mexico

Manuka smoked trout

with tomato caper compote and almond, lemon and honey dressing

Serves 4

4 x 120g fillets rainbow trout

2 handfuls Manuka woodchips

2 sprigs fresh coriander

Tomato and caper compote:

1kg plum tomatoes

500ml tomato consommé

6 drops Tabasco sauce

15ml Worcestershire sauce

35g Demerara sugar

150g salted capers

480g cherry tomatoes yellow

480g cherry tomatoes red

Opal basil, basil and mint tip to garnish

Almond, lemon & honey dressing (makes 300ml):

100g almonds, blanched, roasted & coarsely chopped

3tbs lemon thyme fresh

60ml lemon juice

60g dark honey, preferably Manuka

120ml extra virgin olive oil

Brown sugar, salt & pepper to taste

For the compote, cook the plum tomato and consommé slowly to a purée, stirring to ensure it does not stick to the base of the pan. Remove from the heat and pass through a coarse sieve. Discard the solids. Transfer the liquid back to the original pot, and cook until reduced to about 200ml. Pass through a fine sieve, again discarding the solids. Add the Tabasco and Worcestershire sauces and sugar to taste and allow to cool. Quarter both lots of cherry tomatoes and add together with the capers. Garnish with the opal basil, basil and mint leaves when serving.

To make the dressing, pound the almonds in a mortar and pestle to a chunky and coarse consistency: this gives a nice nutty texture to the dressing. Add the thyme, lemon juice and honey – Manuka honey provides a distinctive strong caramel flavour and rich amber colour. Slowly whisk in the extra virgin olive oil.

Fillet the trout, taking care to remove all bones, then tie the fillets together in pairs with string, having placed a sprig of coriander inside each pair. Sprinkle the trout with the brown sugar, salt and pepper, and shred the Manuka into finger sized strips: two handfuls are enough for anything up to 10 portions of trout. Put the wood chips into the smoker (or on a baking tray in the oven) with the seasoned fish on the grill above the chips. Start at 200°C for 2-3 minutes to get a strong scent of Manuka, then turn the oven down to 150°C for a further 7-8 minutes to allow a slow consistent cooking. This results in a beautiful caramel colour and tender pink centres

To serve, spoon compote into the centre of each plate. Remove the string and separate the trout into individual serving portions on the compote. Drizzle with the dressing.

HUKA LODGE

Taupo, New Zealand

Pan seared scallop and foie gras

with port wine reduction and quince compote

Serves 4

4 x 50g portions Grade A duck foie gras

4 large dry packed diver sea scallops

3 quince, peeled and diced

2tbs sugar

175ml dessert wine
(mild muscat or late harvest sauvignon blanc)

2tbs neutral fruit glaze (or pectin)

375ml port wine

Salt & pepper

Place the diced quince in a shallow pan on a low heat and coat with sugar, salt and pepper. When the juices from the quince are released add the dessert wine and continue to cook on a low heat for 10-15 minutes until the quince is soft and the liquid is almost gone. In a separate pan bring the fruit glaze and an equal amount of water to the boil: coat the quince mixture with the fruit glaze and transfer to a separate container to cool.

Reduce the port in a saucepan over a medium-low heat until it coats the back of a spoon.

Sear the foie gras on all sides in a hot, dry pan, then sear the scallops in the fat that the foie gras leaves behind, making sure not to burn the foie gras fat.

Place a tablespoon of the quince compote on the center of the plate. Drizzle port wine reduction around the compote and arrange a scallop on top of the quince with foie gras on top of the scallop. Shown here with a garnish of halved figs and fried leeks.

INN AT MONTCHANIN VILLAGE

Montchanin, Delaware, USA

Braised beef short ribs

Serves 4

4 x 5cm 4-bone short ribs of beef
2 medium yellow onions, roughly chopped
1 large carrot, roughly chopped
3 sticks celery, roughly chopped
1 bulb garlic cut in half
500ml beef stock
250ml red wine
125ml sherry vinegar
100g chopped tomatoes
1tbs fresh oregano, chopped

Basic brine:
5 litres water
2 cups brown sugar
2 cups kosher salt
2 bay leaves
10 juniper berries

Bring all the ingredients for the brine to the boil in a heavy gauge pot, then leave to cool. When the liquid is cool immerse the ribs for 1 hour (this can be done up to 2 days ahead), then remove from the brine and pat dry.

Sear the short ribs to a golden brown over a medium heat on a barbecue grill (this also can be done a day in advance). In a braising pan caramelise the vegetables, add the wine and reduce until almost dry, then add the beef stock and sherry vinegar. Place the ribs into this liquid, bring to a simmer, cover and place in a preheated oven at 150°C for 3 hours until tender. Remove the ribs from the pan and strain the braising liquid into a medium saucepan. Add the tomato and reduce over a medium-high heat until the sauce coats the back of a spoon. Stir in the chopped oregano and serve over the ribs.

INN AT SOUTHBRIDGE
St Helena, California, USA

Grilled sea bass fillet with Santorini vegetables

Serves 4

4 sea bass fillets, 200g each

100g sundried tomatoes

16 cherry tomatoes, halved

4 courgettes, halved

1 aubergine, cubed

200g white mushrooms

1 each red, yellow, & orange peppers, sliced

Olive paste

Mint

Oregano

Olive oil

Juice of 1 lemon

Marinade:

100ml extra virgin olive oil

Fresh mint

Oregano

Salt & pepper

This dish emphasises the Greek tradition of fresh ingredients from local suppliers, cooked and processed as little as possible to preserve and highlight their natural flavors and aromas.

Wash, trim, and prepare the vegetables. Blend the marinade and immerse the fish and vegetables in it for an hour to absorb the flavors. Grill the marinated fillets and vegetables separately. Cook the vegetables until well browned: the fillets should be moist inside and charred and crispy on the outside.

Make a bed of vegetables with the sea bass on top. Spread a little olive paste – a few olives crushed with a little oil and seasoning – over the fillet. Pour over a dressing of equal parts virgin olive oil mixed with freshly squeezed lemon juice, and decorate with a whole sun-dried tomato on top of the fillet: if available, spike an olive leaf into the tomato. Spill finely chopped mint, oregano, and sun-dried tomatoes all around the dish, with a final drizzle of olive oil.

KATIKIES

Santorini, Greece

SMALL LUXURY RECIPES PAGES 86 - 123

Konju kallappam: Tiger prawns with rice pancakes

The kallappam (rice cakes) should be started a day in advance

Serves 2

8 tiger prawns, about 125g each

6tbs coconut oil

2-3 sprigs curry leaf

300g onion, sliced

50g ginger, cut into thin strips

10 cloves garlic, chopped

3 green chilli, chopped

2.5tbs chilli powder

2tsp turmeric powder

2tsp coriander powder

10 black peppercorns, crushed

Coconut milk

2 small tomatoes, quartered

Salt

Marinade: roast very lightly and grind to a fine powder

8 clove

4 cinnamon sticks

6 green cardamom pods

10g whole cumin seeds

For the kallappam:

200g white raw rice flour

20g sugar

Salt to taste

250ml toddy
(fermented palm tree sap: use coconut milk with 0.5tsp of cooking soda if unavailable)

Soak the raw rice flour in double its volume of water for 4 hours: this will make a very fine paste. Take one cup of the paste and add 4 cups of water; heat this in a saucepan for ten minutes, stirring continuously, then leave the cooked mixture to cool. Once cool, mix the cooked mixture back into the rice paste together with the sugar, salt and toddy, then leave at room temperature to ferment for a minimum of 12 hours, preferably overnight.

Clean, de-vein and wash the prawns, then coat them with half the ground spice marinade. Heat the coconut oil and sauté the curry leaves, onion, ginger, garlic and green chilli. Add the chilli powder, turmeric and coriander and sauté for a further 5-6 minutes until the onion and spices mixture turns brown. Add the marinated prawns and salt to taste, together with the remaining ground spice mixture, then pour in a little coconut milk and cook on a slow heat until the prawns are cooked through. Add the crushed peppercorns and tomato wedges and cook dry.

Before cooking the pancakes check the seasoning and consistency of the batter, which should be light and pouring: add a little coconut milk if you need to thin it down. Heat a non stick pan and pour out 50g of the mixture into a disc, cover and cook for a minute.

To serve, arrange the prawns alongside the hot pancakes with a garnish of shredded vegetables.

KUMARAKOM LAKE RESORT

Kottayam, Kerala, India

Ceviche of cod with yabbies

steamed over lemongrass and limes

Serves 6

LAKE HOUSE

Daylesford, Victoria, Australia

Slice the fish diagonally across the fillet into even slices 5mm thick. Blend the lime juice with the fish sauce and coat the fish with the dressing, ensuring a good overall coverage. Lay the fish slices on a tray, pour over any remaining dressing, cover and refrigerate for two hours.

Sweat the lemongrass, ginger, onions and chilli in a little oil over a medium heat until the onions are soft. Add the coconut milk and simmer for 15 minutes, then remove from the heat and allow to cool. When cool, purée and pass through a fine sieve, discarding the residue.

Drain the lime sauce from the pre-marinated fish and coat the slices generously with the cold coconut dressing. Leave to marinate for a further two hours in the refrigerator, reserving the excess dressing.

Make a dressing for the yabbies by blending the lime juice, fish sauce, palm sugar and mint in a bowl. Put the live yabbies in the freezer for five minutes to anaesthetize them: meanwhile set up a steamer, scattering the sliced lime, lemongrass and lime leaves over the base of the steamer basket. Steam the yabbies a few at a time over rapidly boiling water for two to three minutes, then plunge them into iced water to stop them cooking further. Using small sharp scissors, cut open the shell along the back, remove the intestinal tract and rinse under cold running water. Pat them dry and partially peel back the shell to expose the tail meat. Crack the claws. Dry the yabbies well and toss them in the dressing.

Remove six large leaves from the lettuce and slice the remainder into thin strips. Lay one large lettuce leaf into each of six cocktail glasses. Lightly coat the shredded lettuce with the reserved coconut dressing and distribute amongst the cocktail glasses. Top with slices of ceviche and hang two yabbies on the rim of each glass, garnishing with small strips of iced chilli, a quarter of lime, and puffed rice noodles: serve immediately.

Ceviche:

1 fillet of fish 800g - 1kg
We use locally farmed Murray cod but any firm white fleshed fish can be substituted

600ml fresh lime juice

1tsp fish sauce

Coconut dressing:

1 stalk of lemongrass, sliced

1 knob ginger, peeled & diced

1 Spanish onion, peeled and sliced.

2 birdseye chillies, seeded and diced

1 tin coconut milk

Yabbies:

12 live yabbies (freshwater crayfish)

3 kaffir lime leaves

Half a lime, thinly sliced

Two stalks of lemongrass, roughly chopped & bruised

3tsp fresh lime juice

1tsp fish sauce

1 small knob palm sugar

4 leaves fresh mint, finely chopped

To finish:

Half an iceberg lettuce

One and a half limes, cut into quarters

6 small red chillies sliced lengthwise and placed in iced water

12-18 rice noodles fried in hot oil until puffed and crisp

Duck breast tournedos with Sarlat potatoes

Serves 4

2 duck breasts (magrets) of 450g each

3 sheets of filo pastry

50g butter

1kg potatoes

250g cèpes mushrooms

1 clove garlic

3tsp chopped parsley

A day in advance, take off and keep all the fat from the two duck breasts. Melt the butter and use it to lightly coat the sheets of pastry. Lay out the sheets on top of each other, place the duck breasts on top, and wrap the breasts tightly to make a large duck cylinder. Wrap the cylinder in paper and store it in the fridge.

On the day, peel, wash and slice the potatoes. Gently clean the cèpes with a wet cloth and cut them into blades. Chop the garlic and parsley separately. In a shallow casserole, brown the potatoes in the duck fat until they are slightly coloured, then add the cèpes and continue cooking, stirring regularly. When the potatoes are cooked add the chopped parsley and garlic.

Cut the duck cylinder into four portions, take off the paper film, and season with salt and pepper. Quickly fry the tournedos, turning them regularly: when the filo is evenly coloured overall transfer to the oven at 170°C to finish; 5 minutes for rare, 15 for well done. Serve as shown.

LE MANOIR DE BELLERIVE

Dordogne, France

Tomato red curried tiger prawns

with aubergine temparadu and boiled country rice

Serves 2

400g tiger prawns

3tsp coconut oil (or vegetable if unavailable)

50g garlic, chopped

150g onions, chopped

50g ginger, cut in thin strips

5g cinnamon

1 bunch curry leaves

3tsp red chilli powder

1.5tsp curry powder

200g tomato, seeded & chopped

1.5tsp salt

125ml water

Temparadu:

2 aubergines

2 whole capsicums

2 rings from a large onion

1tsp turmeric powder

5g mustard seeds

30g garlic, chopped

100g onions, chopped

30g ginger

5g cinnamon

2tsp curry powder

0.5tsp black pepper, crushed

1tsp mustard cream

2 green chillies

1tsp salt

3tsp coconut oil (or vegetable if unavailable)

125ml thick coconut milk

1 bunch curry leaves

1cm pandan leaf

80g red country rice

80g white country rice

1tsp salt

Wash and cook the two rices separately. Add salt and water to 2cm deeper than the rice level and bring both pans to the boil. Reduce the heat and simmer until the rice is tender.

For the temparadu halve the aubergines, then cut each half lengthways into four 'fingers' while keeping the vegetable connected at the stem. Marinate the aubergine, capsicums and onion rings with a pinch of salt and a quarter of the turmeric powder, then deep fry in hot vegetable oil for two minutes and set aside. Heat the coconut oil in a pan and sauté the mustard seeds, garlic, onion, ginger and cinnamon; add the curry powder, the remaining turmeric powder, crushed pepper and mustard cream and continue, stirring frequently, for a further 3-4 minutes. Finally add the fried aubergine, onion rings, capsicum and the coconut milk and cook for a further 5-6 minutes, adjusting the seasoning before serving.

Mix together the chilli powder, curry powder and salt and coat the prawns with half of the mix, then leave them to marinate. Meanwhile heat the oil and sauté the garlic, onion, ginger, cinnamon and curry leaves for 4 minutes. Add the rest of the chilli and curry powder and cook for a further 2 minutes, then add the chopped tomato and water and boil for another 7 minutes. Put the prawns in the pan and continue until they are cooked through. Check the seasoning before serving.

Serve as shown. Press the red and white rice half and half into a mould and turn out the mould onto the plate.

LIGHTHOUSE HOTEL & SPA

Dadella, Galle, Sri Lanka

Goose in the pan

with apple salad and 'first of season' artichokes

Serves 4

1 goose

2 litres goose fat

100g Guérande salt

50g spring onions, cut into strips

1 Granny Smith apple

100g mixed salad leaves
(eg spinach, coriander, frisée, rocket)

2 castaure (first of season globe artichokes)

Olive oil

Freshly baked crusty bread

Bone the goose, separating the thighs from the breast; you can ask your butcher to do this for you. Score the breast skin lightly with a knife and set out all the meat sprinkled with the salt and the spring onions. Let it rest for at least 12 hours, then drain off the fat. Put each lean breast or thigh piece into an airtight plastic bag, then fill the bag with goose fat, making sure there are no air bubbles, and seal tight. Cook in a steam oven at 85°C, or over boiling water on a grill in the oven, until the meat is cooked through (about 30 minutes).

Cool the bags with iced water and take the fat off the meat, then cut the breasts into thin slices. Fry the thighs in oil until browned, and season the salad leaves. Wash the artichokes and cut and lightly fry eight thin slices. In a terrine mould layer the salad, warm thigh meat, a thin layer of apple, bread crusts and fried artichoke slices. Serve cold goose breast slices on the plate alongside the turned out 'confit cake': a cup of smoky Lapsang Souchong tea is the perfect accompaniment.

LONDRA PALACE

Venice, Italy

Canon of roe deer

with a potato, black pudding and shallot torte, asparagus mousse and sautéed chanterelles

Serves 4

Heat the olive oil until smoking, then seal the roe deer fillets, season, and set on a plate to cool.

Blend the chicken breast, egg, and cream in a processor to form a mousse; season and place in a clean bowl in the fridge. Sauté three quarters of the chanterelles in butter, remove from the pan, chop finely and leave to cool. Finely chop the parsley and pick the thyme leaves; when the chanterelles are cold add them together with the herbs to the mousse. Check the seasoning.

Lay two slices of Parma ham on a piece of cling film and spread the mousse evenly over the ham. Place a fillet of roe deer on top and wrap the cling film tightly to form a sausage shape: repeat for all four fillets, wrap the sausages individually in foil for protection and store in the fridge until required.

THE MARCLIFFE AT PITFODELS

Aberdeen, Scotland

Roast the canons in their foil in a moderate oven (170°C) for 15-20 minutes. Remove to a warm place to rest for ten minutes, then remove the foil and film and slice into three equal pieces.

To make the torte bring the butter and chicken stock to the boil in a pan, removing from the heat when they have emulsifed. Peel and wash the potatoes and cut into thinly sliced discs – as thin as possible – preferably with a mandolin. Toss the potato slices in the emulsified stock and place over heat for five minutes to wilt but not cook the slices. Peel, finely shred, and sauté the shallots in the olive oil until slightly coloured. Season well, drain in a colander and set aside.

Place a 20cm flan ring on a baking sheet and arrange the sliced potatoes inside the flan ring, overlapping the lip. After two layers of potato, crumble the black pudding and spread it evenly over the potatoes; repeat with the sautéed shallots. Finish with a layer of potatoes in a scalloped effect and season. Transfer to a 150°C oven and cook for 40 minutes, pressing down every ten minutes to prevent burning. When cooked, remove from the oven, place another tray on top and lightly press the torte.

To prepare the mousse, peel the asparagus and blanch in boiling water for four minutes, then remove and refresh in iced water to retain the colour. Heat the cream with the garlic and white wine, then place asparagus and cream in a liquidiser and purée until smooth. Pass through a sieve into a clean bowl, then add the egg and whisk, checking the seasoning.

To make the jus, sauté the shallots and trimmings in the butter to a deep brown colour. Add the pimento berries, mace, and cloves. Deglaze the pan with the wine and reduce to a syrupy consistency. Add both stocks and bring to the boil; skim, and add the bay leaves. Reduce the stock to a third, season, pass through a muslim cloth, and place in a clean pan ready to serve.

To serve, arrange the canons of roe deer on a plate with the torte and the mousse as shown: drizzle with the jus.

Canon of roe deer:

Four 170g fillets of roe deer (save the trimmings for the jus)

1 chicken suprême

1 egg white

8 fine slices Parma ham

230g fresh chanterelles

500g chopped fresh flat parsley

1 pinch nutmeg

2 sprigs thyme

50g butter

300ml double cream

Torte:

8 potatoes

340g butter

1 litre good chicken stock

1.5tbs olive oil

8 shallots

110g black pudding

Mousse:

230g asparagus

1.5 eggs

1.5 egg yolks

150ml double cream

Half a clove garlic, crushed

100ml white wine

Jus:

300ml game stock

300ml chicken stock

6 pimento berries, crushed

2 cloves

1 blade mace

2 bay leaves

50g butter

4 shallots, chopped

1 glass cabernet sauvignon

Roe deer trimmings

Halibut spring roll

with cashew nut and fresh pea sauce

Serves 4

4 x 200g halibut fillets

1tsp sesame oil

1tsp red curry paste

50ml soya sauce

1tsp sunflower oil

100g leek julienne

100g carrots julienne

50g fresh celery leaves

100g fresh soybean sprouts

10g sugar

Salt

4 pieces spring roll pastry 25cm x 25cm

30g melted butter

For the sauce:

180g fresh peas, boiled

50g cashew nuts

120ml chicken stock

80ml soy sauce

50g cold butter

Blend the curry paste and the 50ml of soy sauce with a little salt, then coat the cleaned fillets with the mixture and leave for 5 minutes to marinate. Fry the fish in sesame oil in a hot pan for about one and a half minutes each side for medium done.

In a very hot pan quickly fry the leek, carrot, celery and bean sprouts in the sunflower oil. Add sugar and salt to the fried vegetables, then divide them into four portions on the laid out spring roll pastry. Arrange the fish over the vegetables and close the spring roll by bringing opposite corners together: be careful that the pastry does not break. Brush the pastry with melted butter and bake for 10 minutes in the oven at 210°C.

Meanwhile briefly fry the peas and the cashews in a pan, then after a few seconds add the soy sauce and chicken stock. Cook until half the liquid is left, then transfer to a bowl and whip the sauce with the cold butter until it becomes creamy.

Arrange the pea and cashew sauce in the middle of a warm plate: slice the fish pastry once down the middle and position it on the top of the sauce.

MINOS BEACH ART'OTEL

Aghios Nikolaos, Crete, Greece

Bill Beane, photogra

Crab cakes

with orange, mango and green peppercorn marmalade

Serves 4

Crab cakes:

500g jumbo lump crabmeat, picked & cleaned

250ml tartare sauce

50g pickled jalepeño peppers, finely chopped

2 large eggs, beaten

1tbs Dijon mustard

1tbs Worcestershire sauce

50g each onion, green onion & red pepper, finely chopped

100g panko bread crumbs

Olive oil

Marmalade:

200g orange marmalade

50ml apple cider vinegar

50g diced red onion

50g diced red pepper

75g canned whole green peppercorns, drained

1tsp ground allspice

Half a green onion, chopped

2 ripe mangos peeled and cut to a 5mm dice

4 young soft-shell crabs, cleaned

1 egg

Preheat the oven to 180°C. In a large bowl mix all the ingredients except the crabmeat until well combined, then add the meat, gently folding it in to avoid breaking the lumps. Form 4 cakes using a round mould: chill until very firm. Heat a little oil over a medium heat in an ovenproof pan. Sauté the crab cakes until they are light brown on each side, then transfer the crab cakes to the oven for about 15 minutes.

Place all ingredients for the marmalade except the green onion and half the mango in a large saucepan. Slowly simmer over a medium heat for 10 minutes, then remove from the heat and add the green onion and remaining mango.

Season the soft shell crabs well and dip them in the beaten egg mixed with a little water or milk. Fry them in oil for 3-5 minutes until they are brown and crisp.

To serve, ladle marmalade onto the plate and place a crab cake in the centre with a fried crab anchored to it by a small wooden skewer. Decorate around the crab cakes with droplets of beurre blanc and garnish with fried curls of beet.

MONMOUTH PLANTATION

Natchez, Mississippi, USA

Picnic muesli

Makes 12 portions

750g bran flakes

500g rolled oats

250g sunflower seeds

500g clear honey

125ml sunflower oil

2tbs ground cinnamon

A handful of chopped nuts

A handful of whole cashews

A handful dried mango

A handful of dried coconut

A handful of raisins

Preheat the oven to 200°C. Crumble the bran flakes into a roasting pan and add the rolled oats and sunflower seeds. Mix well. In a bowl, combine the honey, sunflower oil and cinnamon. Stir the honey mixture thoroughly into the oat mixture until the cereal and seeds are evenly coated. Bake, stirring occasionally, until the muesli turns golden brown.

Allow to cool then fold in the other ingredients.

Store in an airtight container for up to a month. Fill picnic glasses with full cream vanilla yoghurt, top with the muesli, drizzle with macadamia nut honey and top with fresh strawberries.

Add one game ranger with iced cocktails and an awe-inspiring view.

NGALA PRIVATE GAME RESERVE

South Africa

NUKUBATI ISLAND

Labasa, Fiji

Baked Fijian mud crab with coconut cream

Serves 4

4 mud crabs
We use male crabs, fresh from Nukubati's mangroves

2 tomatoes

1 white onion

1 red onion

1 hot red chilli

1 lemon

4 fresh mature coconuts

Juice of 1 lemon

1 bunch coriander

4 spring onion

Salt & pepper

Steam the crabs in a wok, then leave to cool. Extract all the flesh – we use male crabs because the flesh is easier to remove – and put it in a large bowl. Keep the shell and large claws backs. Add finely chopped tomatoes, onions and chilli to the flesh, squeeze over the juice from the lemon and leave to stand while preparing the fresh coconut cream.

Break open the 4 coconuts and save the coconut water. Grate and divide the flesh into 2 equal halves. Add 2 cups of coconut water to one half and knead this mixture thoroughly, then squeeze through a muslin cloth to make the coconut cream. Add the lemon juice and season to taste. Fold into the crab meat and spoon the mixture into the 4 crab shells. Cover each shell with foil, place on a baking tray, and bake in the oven at 150°C for 15 minutes.

Add half a cup of coconut water to the second half of the grated coconut flesh, knead the mixture thoroughly, and squeeze it through a muslin cloth into a clean bowl. This makes a richer thicker coconut cream, which is topped onto the crab in the shell. Return the crabs to the oven for a final 5 minutes.

Remove the baked crabs from the oven and arrange on plates garnished with coriander leaves and shredded spring onions. Serve hot in the shell with side dishes of kawai fries (local wild yams) and lightly sautéed pumpkin shoots.

Ceviche of Pacific scallops

with tomato vierge and kalamata olive tapenade

Serves 4

Ceviche:

12 scallops, roe removed

2 shallots, finely diced

Juice of 1 lemon

2tbs diced cucumber

1tbs extra virgin olive oil

1 litre fish stock

4 bread sticks

Herb oil:

Half a bunch rocket, chopped

1 cup chopped soft herbs (eg basil, parsley, chervil, chives)

Pinch of saffron

Grated rind from 1 lemon

1 clove garlic, crushed

1 shallot, chopped

1tbs grated Parmesan

250ml extra virgin olive oil

Tapenade:

4tbs pitted kalamata olives

1tbs grated Parmesan

1tbs baby capers

2 anchovy fillets, chopped

1 clove garlic, chopped

1tbs parsley, chopped

Grated rind of 1 lemon

1tbs olive oil

Tomato vierge:

6 vine ripened tomatoes, skinned, seeded, and diced

2tbs chopped chives

2tbs diced red onion

2tbs chopped parsley

1 clove garlic, chopped

1tbs coriander seeds, roasted & crushed

1tbs extra virgin olive oil

1tbs white balsamic vinegar

Bring the fish stock to the boil and blanch the scallops for 30 seconds, then immediately refresh them in iced water. Slice the scallops into wafer thin pieces, mix with the remaining ceviche ingredients and marinate for at least 4 hours.

To prepare the herb oil blanch the rocket and herbs for 10 seconds in boiling water, then refresh immediately in iced water. Drain and squeeze out any excess liquid. Using a hand blender, combine all the other ingredients with half the olive oil: the saffron dramatically increases the density of the colour. Add the blanched herbs a little at a time while blending, then add the remaining oil and adjust the seasoning.

Chop the olives to a coarse paste, then sir in the remaining tapenade ingredients and adjust the seasoning. The tapenade should be firm enough to hold its shape when spooned out.

Mix together all the ingredients for the tomato vierge a few minutes before serving to allow all the flavours to infuse.

To serve arrange a square mould in the center of each dish. Fill with the tomato mixture and sprinkle with a little salt and pepper, then neatly arrange the sliced marinated scallops on top of the tomato and remove the mould. Dress the plate with the herb oil, a quenelle of olive tapenade and a bread stick.

THE OBEROI BALI

Depasar, Bali, Indonesia

Crispy skin salmon

dusted with Mauritian spices with an okra, corn and tomato salsa and a carrot, tomato and ginger broth

Serves 4

THE OBEROI MAURITIUS

Pointe aux Piments, Mauritius

To start the broth, sauté the onion and ginger in the olive oil. Bruise the lemongrass with the back of a knife and add it to the pan, then sauté for another minute until the aroma releases. Add the carrot and tomato juices, bring to the boil, and simmer for 20 minutes. Check the seasoning and pass through a fine sieve, then set aside.

Combine all the ingredients for the spice mix: this will be used for seasoning the fish immediately before frying. Wash and clean the greens, then blanch them in boiling water and refresh in iced water. To reheat, brush them with a little melted butter, season, wrap in cling film and cook in the microwave for 30 seconds.

For the salsa, trim the stems from the okra and cut the flesh at an angle to make lozenge shapes. Cut the tomatoes into wedges, remove the seeds, then chop into a small dice. Blanch the sweet corn in boiling water, then refresh. Add the olive oil to a hot pan and sauté the garlic for 1 minute, then add the okra and sauté for 3 to 4 minutes. Take off the heat and stir in the tomato and sweetcorn. Adjust the consistency and seasoning with a little more olive oil and salt and pepper.

Dust the salmon fillets on both sides with the spice mix and pour a little olive oil into a hot non-stick pan. When the oil begins to smoke, cook the salmon fillets skin side down for about 2 minutes. Turn the fillets over and cook for a further 4 to 5 minutes on a lower heat – the cooking time will vary depending on the thickness of the fillet. Divide the salsa onto serving plates: reheat the greens and arrange in the centre of each plate. Spoon carrot and tomato sauce into the bowl and place the fillet on top of the Asian greens. Finish with a flourish of deep fried vegetable strips on top of the salmon.

4 x 160g salmon fillets

4 choi sum, kai lan or similar Asian greens

Broth:

50g onion, finely diced

1 ginger root, peeled & crushed to a paste

50ml olive oil

6 lemongrass stems, bruised

500ml carrot juice

500ml tomato juice

Spice mix:

5g/1tsp sweet paprika

5g/1tsp coriander powder

5g/1tsp black pepper

5g/1tsp turmeric

10g/2tsp orange powder

Salsa:

200g okra

120g sweetcorn kernels

200g vine ripened tomatoes

3g garlic, peeled & chopped

5g chives, washed & chopped

100ml olive oil

Garnish:

20g deep fried fine strips of vegetables (leek, carrot, celery leaves)

Spicy steamed barramundi

served with roasted aubergine and choy tam

Serves 4

PANGKOR LAUT ISLAND

Lumut, Malaysia

4 x 180g barramundi fillets, skin on and trimmed

320g aubergine, soft oven roasted

Sea salt & white pepper

Corn oil

Spicy sauce:

1tbs lemongrass, finely chopped

1tbs ginger flowers, finely chopped

1tbs birdseye chilli, finely chopped

1tbs fresh turmeric, finely chopped

1tbs pickled leek, finely chopped

1tbs tangerine juice

0.5tbs tangerine zest

1tbs Thai chilli sauce
Mae Pranom is the best brand

1tbs fine salt

Chilli oil:

15g dried chili

2tbs corn oil

Coriander oil:

80g fresh coriander leaves

2tbs corn oil

Pumpkin sauce:

240g pumpkin

500ml water

Pinch of salt

Garnish:

160g fresh baby choy tam

1tbs chopped smoked garlic

Blanch the coriander leaves in lightly salted boiling water, then immerse in iced water, squeeze out all moisture, and blend with the corn oil until it is a fine coulis. Leave to infuse for 8 hours, then strain.

Combine all the ingredients for the spicy sauce except the tangerine juice and Thai chilli sauce and leave at room temperature. When the chopped ingredients have become soft - after about 20 minutes - add the Thai chilli sauce and tangerine juice and blend till smooth, then season with dried chilli oil, prepared by heating the corn oil and cooking the dried chilli until it turns dark brown, then taking it off the stove and leave at room temperature to cool.

Boil the pumpkin in the lightly salted water. When soft, blend it smooth and pass through a fine sieve.

Halve the aubergine lengthwise, pan fry in corn oil until coloured, then roast in the oven at 170°C until soft. Blanch the choy tam, then lightly fry in corn oil with the chopped garlic. Season the fish, coat in corn oil, then place in a hot steamer for 8-10 minutes.

Place the aubergine in the center of the plate. Arrange the steamed fish on top, lightly covered with spicy sauce. Garnish with the fried vegetables lightly sprinkled with dried chilli oil, coriander oil and pumpkin sauce.

Poached monkfish 'Façon Côte d'Azur', bourride de lotte á l'antiboise

Serves 6

1kg monkfish fillet

18 Manila clams

18 black mussels

1 pinch saffron

1 Idaho potato

3 small leeks

700g fresh fava beans

3 vine ripened tomatoes

6 shallots, finely chopped

8 garlic cloves

1 sprig each fresh thyme, tarragon, rosemary

1 bay leaf

A half-bunch Italian parsley

1 sprig fresh basil

475ml white wine

4 tablespoons olive oil

Aioli:

(110g mashed Idaho potato)

2 egg yolks

475ml extra virgin olive oil

2 garlic cloves, chopped

1 pinch saffron

Juice of 1 lemon

Sea salt & freshly ground pepper

Wash, peel, and cut the potato into thick slices. In a pan add enough water to cover the potatoes, sea salt, the bay leaf, a pinch of saffron, and 2 crushed garlic cloves. Cook until tender and drain, reserving the saffron water. Mash and set aside the potato.

Wash and cut the leeks into 2cm slices, then cook in full boiling water until tender. Refresh and set aside. Peel the fava beans, cook for 2 minutes in full boiling water, refresh, remove the skin and set aside. Wash the tomato, blanch in boiling water for 30 seconds, refresh in iced water, remove the skin, dice and set aside.

Gently warm 3 tablespoons of olive oil in a pan with a lid, then add the diced shallots, 6 crushed cloves of garlic, thyme, tarragon and rosemary. Add the Manila clams, mussels, white wine, and freshly ground pepper, cover, and cook over a high heat until the shells open. Remove and set the shellfish aside: keep the cooking liquid.

To prepare the aioli mix together the egg yolks and mashed potato, whisking in the olive oil slowly as if making mayonnaise. Add the chopped garlic, lemon juice, and a pinch of saffron, then set aside.

Before serving, pour the mussel broth and potato saffron water into a heavy based pan. Bring the liquid to the boil and poach the seasoned fish in it for 8 to 10 minutes, then add all the cooked vegetables, clams and mussels. Spoon the fish and vegetables into a large soup bowl, then strain the cooking broth into a bowl and, using a hand blender, combine with half of the aioli: the broth must be foamy. Serve as shown.

TAPENADE RESTAURANT, HOTEL PARISI

La Jolla, California, USA

Veal tasting menu

Veal medallion with chanterelles and Madeira, veal sweetbread with rosemary brown butter, and braised veal bacon

Serves 4

POST RANCH INN

Big Sur, California, USA

Veal medallion:

4 x 70g medallions of veal tenderloin

25g clarified butter

3 shallots

2 sprigs thyme

250ml veal demi-glace or reduced veal/chicken stock

200ml Madeira

1tbs black truffle purée

200g chanterelle mushrooms, cleaned

Veal sweetbreads:

4 x 50g veal sweetbread

Flour for dusting

Salt & pepper

50g clarified butter

50g whole butter

1tsp capers

1tsp crushed garlic

1tsp lemon juice

Rosemary

Braised veal bacon:

4 pieces veal bacon

1 litre chicken stock

1 apple, diced and caramelised

Sauce:

250ml port

250ml red wine

250ml chicken stock

100g sugar

1 cinnamon stick

Medallions

Sweat the shallots in the butter in a saucepan, then add the thyme and Madeira. Reduce the liquid by two thirds, then add the demi-glace. Simmer for 10 minutes and strain. Sauté the chanterelles until lightly caramelised, then add to the sauce with the black truffle purée and season to taste.

Sear the veal medallions on both sides.

Sweetbreads

Dredge the sweetbreads in seasoned flour and sauté in clarified butter. When brown, drain off all the oil and add the whole butter. When the butter starts to brown, add first the garlic and capers, then the lemon juice and a sprig of rosemary. Adjust the seasoning.

Braised veal bacon

Brown the bacon slowly in oil – about 15 minutes per side – in an ovenproof pan. Add the chicken stock, cover, and place in the oven at 150°C for 2 hours.

For the sauce, bring the port, red wine, chicken stock and thyme to the boil and reduce to a thick syrup.

Serve all three together on the plate: a medallion with its sauce spooned over and a sweetbread with its sauce, garnished with a sprig of rosemary. Cut the bacon into cubes and arrange a small mound on each plate, topped with caramelised apples, drizzled with port syrup, and garnished with a sprig of thyme.

Potato purée and sautéed baby squash:

2 russet potatoes

2 Yukon gold potatoes

125ml double cream

100g butter

8 baby courgettes

50ml veal or chicken stock

Boil the peeled and cubed potatoes in salted water until done, then drain and put through a food mill with the butter. Warm and fold in the cream; check and adjust the seasoning. Lightly sauté the courgettes in olive oil and a little stock: season to taste. Slice and arrange on the plate, with puréed potato on top.

Costa Rican 'Casado'

Casado is one of the classic dishes of Costa Rica. The name literally means married man, and according to tradition is what he should expect to receive after he gets married. It is served by portions on a large plate.

Serves 1

200g red snapper fillet
10g fresh dill
150g rice
2 red peppers, chopped
50g chopped onion
150g black beans
1 head garlic
150g butter
10g celery, diced
150g diced vegetables of your choosing
25g sweet corn
120g sweet plantains
25g red cabbage, chopped
2 carrots
1 large tomato
10g fresh coriander leaves
Juice from 1 lemon
Olive oil
Salt & pepper
50g white cheese to garnish
1 fried egg to top off cooked vegetables
2 corn tortillas to wrap fish and vegetables in

Season the fish with salt, pepper and fresh dill, then cook in olive oil for about 5 minutes on each side. Wash the rice. In a frying pan brown one of the peppers and half the chopped onion, then add the rice with 500ml water and salt and pepper to taste. Cover and bring to the boil, then reduce the temperature and continue cooking until all of the water is absorbed.

Wash the beans and bring them to the boil in 750ml of water with a head of garlic, the rest of the chopped onion, and the celery. Check the seasoning and let the pan boil until the beans are soft, then drain. For the diced vegetable salad, brown the remaining sweet pepper and onion in the butter in a frying pan with celery, garlic and your vegetables of choice. Add salt and pepper to taste, then add the sweet corn and cook for about 20 minutes. Cut the plantains into thick slices and flatten these into discs, then fry in olive oil until browned on both sides.

Finely chop the red cabbage, carrots, tomato and coriander. Add olive oil, salt, pepper and lemon juice and toss. Serve on a corn tortilla, garnished with white cheese and a fried egg.

HOTEL PUNTA ISLITA
Guanacaste, Costa Rica

Seared yellowfin tuna

Serves 2

2 x 160gm Tuna steak

140g wild risotto rice

60g saffron fumet

40g tomato salsa

30g wakame (edible seaweed)

2 cloves garlic, chopped

1tsp sweet paprika

2tsp olive oil

10g basil oil

Marinate the tuna steaks with salt, pepper and sweet paprika for at least 2 hours. Heat a little olive oil in a pan, then sear the tuna steak until medium. Heat up the saffron fumet, then sauté the wakame in the stock with the chopped garlic: check seasoning.

Serve the tuna steak over the cooked wild risotto rice, topped with the wilted wakame. Pour the saffron fumet and tomato salsa around the tuna, then drizzle with basil oil.

PURI WULANDARI

Ubud-Gianyar, Bali, Indonesia

Fresh tuna steak

tomato maize, mango and fresh chilli pepper chutney

Serves 10

2kg fresh tuna cut into steaks

Maize bread,
toasted and made into fine breadcrumbs

100ml extra virgin olive oil

Sea salt & ground black pepper

Fried maize:

500g corn flour

50g butter

500g peeled tomatoes

Chutney:

500g fresh mangoes, peeled & stoned

50g mascovado (rich, dark & spicy) sugar

1 fresh chilli pepper, seeded and chopped

50ml sugar cane rum

5 whole black peppercorns, crushed

10ml lemon juice

60g rocket lettuce

Coriander leaves

For the fried maize dissolve the flour in a little water and keep to one side. Separately, bring the butter and tomatoes to the boil in 2.2 litres of water. Season with sea salt, then add the flour mixture when boiling. Take off the boil, stirring continuously. Put onto a greased baking tray and allow to cool. Cut the solidified mixture into cubes about 2cm square, deep-fry the cubes in hot oil, and drain on kitchen paper.

To prepare the chutney heat the mangoes with the muscovado sugar and allow them to caramelise. Add the chilli pepper, rum, and pepper. Leave to cool, seasoning with sea salt and a dash of fresh lemon juice.

Season each tuna steak with sea salt and the ground black pepper, cover with the breadcrumbs and cook in hot oil until browned both sides. Put in the oven at 200°C for ten minutes to finish off.

To serve, arrange the fried maize in the middle of the plate with the tuna on top and the chutney to the side. Finish with a bouquet of rocket and fresh coriander on the tuna.

QUINTA DA CASA BRANCA
Funchal, Madeira, Portugal

THE OBEROI RAJVILAS, JAIPUR

Jaipur, Rajasthan, India

Prawn, crab and leek ravioli with sauce vierge

Serves 4

Pasta dough:

250g flour

2 whole eggs

2 egg yolks

15ml extra virgin olive oil

Pinch of fine sea salt

Ravioli filling:

250g white crab meat

150g leeks

Chopped thyme

15g unsalted butter

Salt and pepper to taste

Prawn mousse:

100g raw tiger prawns, shelled

25g egg white

150ml double cream

To garnish:

1 aubergine skin, shredded and deep-fried

Sauce vierge:

125ml extra virgin olive oil

150g tomatoes, peeled, de-seeded and finely diced

20g parsley

10g dill

25g chervil

Lemon juice to taste

Salt & ground white pepper to taste

Mix the ingredients for the sauce vierge and keep at room temperature for 2-3 hours to allow the flavours to infuse.

To prepare the pasta dough, place all the ingredient in a food processor and blend using the pulse setting until the dough forms a ball. Pass the dough through a pasta roller or roll with a rolling pin. Wrap in cling film and place in the refrigerator for 30 minutes.

For the ravioli filling, sauté the shredded leeks in unsalted butter over a medium heat until tender, season with salt and pepper, and lay out to cool on kitchen paper. Meanwhile chop the tiger prawns and blend to a smooth paste in a food processor, then add the egg white and continue for 3 or 4 seconds until the egg white has blended with the prawn. Using the pulse setting, add the cream a little at a time until combined: do not blend for too long or the cream may curdle. Mix in a bowl with the cold leeks and the white crab meat, add a little chopped thyme, season with salt and pepper and chill until needed.

To assemble the ravioli cut the dough in half and roll through the pasta machine or with a heavy rolling pin till it is about 0.75 mm thick. Using a 7.5cm diameter pastry cutter, cut out 16 discs. Cover these with a moist cloth. Repeat with the other half of the dough, this time with an 8cm cutter to make the tops of the ravioli. Divide the filling evenly between the 16 smaller discs, leaving a 5mm rim around the edge. Moisten the rims with a little water and stick the 8cm discs on top. Seal each ravioli with the finger tips to ensure a tight seal and to prevent opening during cooking. Store the ravioli on flour dusted trays in the refrigerator until needed (they can be made up to 2 hours before serving).

To serve, cook the ravioli in a large pot of boiling water with a little oil and sea salt for 4 minutes. Drain and arrange on the plate, pouring the sauce evenly over and garnishing with shredded and deep fried aubergine skin. Serve at once.

SMALL LUXURY RECIPES PAGES 126 - 163

Stuffed lamb loin

with couscous and a rosemary sauce

Serves 4

1 loin of lamb

10 - 12 vine leaves

6 - 7 sun-dried tomatoes

150g Feta cheese

Olive oil

Green olives

Salt & black pepper

Sauce:

50g butter

Olive oil

2 onions, sliced

125ml red wine

100ml demi-glace (optional)

Flour

2 sprigs rosemary

50g black olives

Salt & black pepper

Couscous:

250g couscous

500ml of water

30g butter

Salt

Parsley for garnish

Lay out the vine leaves on buttered foil. Bone the lamb loin – keep the bones – and spread the meat over the leaves: sprinkle with salt and pepper, add olive oil and place the sun-dried tomatoes, cheese and green olives on top of the meat. Roll up into an even cylinder and firmly wrap with the foil. Place the foil-wrapped meat in a roasting tin, add half a teacup of water, and cook at 200°C for about 40 minutes. After roasting, leave it to rest for about 15 minutes before cutting into slices.

Meanwhile prepare the sauce. Heat the butter and a little olive oil in a saucepan, add the onions, and brown the bones. Remove the bones and the onions, add the red wine and bring to the boil. Finish the sauce with a teaspoon of flour and, for a more intense flavour, demi-glace. Stir continuously as it thickens. When ready, remove the sauce from the heat and pass through a strainer into a clean saucepan. Reheat, adding the black olives and rosemary leaves, and adjust the seasoning.

Cook the couscous according to the instructions. Drain the water from the saucepan and sauté the grains in the butter.

To serve, shape the couscous firmly into a 5-6cm ring or cup and arrange it on the plate with three slices of the lamb loin. Pour the sauce with the olives and rosemary over the meat; decorate with fresh parsley on top of the couscus.

RODOS PARK SUITES HOTEL

Rhodes, Greece

Spicy seafood and vegetable filled rice pastry roll

with quail egg hopper on a lemongrass infused seafood gravy

Serves 8

For the quail egg hopper, mix the raw rice flour and salt in a bowl and add the yeast mixture and coconut milk to make a smooth batter. Cover and set aside to rise for 2 hours. When ready to serve, grease and heat a small round bottom pan over a moderate flame. Pour out a teaspoonful of batter for each hopper and tilt the pan to form a flower shape around the base. Bake till lightly set, then break a quail egg into the centre and continue to cook until golden brown.

Fry the onion, curry leaves and green chillies in the vegetable oil. Add all other ingredients except the fish, potatoes, stock and coconut milk. After a few minutes add the fish, fry for a few more minutes, then add the stock and coconut milk to make a rich gravy. Reserve part of the gravy, and add the potatoes. Cook for a few minutes until the mixture thickens, then use the seafood and vegetable filling to stuff the raw tubes of calamari.

Sieve the red and white rice flour into separate bowls. Add enough boiling water to each to achieve a soft but not sticky consistency. Lay out and seal alternate strips of the two doughs onto baking mats or oil paper. Place stuffed calamari in the middle and carefully wrap and securely seal within the dough. Steam until cooked.

To serve, slice the stuffed roll and neatly arrange on the centre of the plate with a quail egg hopper and oriental salad cups on the side. Pour the reserved gravy around.

Quail egg hopper:

8 quail eggs

100g raw rice flour

2g yeast dissolved in 50ml water

150ml coconut milk

Rice pastry roll :

225g roasted white rice flour

225g roasted red rice flour

5g salt

Seafood and vegetable filling:

250g onion chopped

30g curry powder

30g garlic chopped

25g green chillies

500g mixed vegetables (3 colour peppers, courgettes, celery, carrot and leeks)

3g saffron

1 stick lemon grass

40g salt

10g freshly ground pepper

1.4kg mixed crustaceans & fish

150ml fish stock

150g boiled potatoes

300ml coconut milk

350g calamari tubes

50ml vegetable oil

SAMAN VILLAS

Aturuwella, Bentota, Sri Lanka

Salmon and mullet tandoori

with cumin filo and coriander crushed fennel, basil potatoes and a coulis of Asian spices

Serves 2

125g salmon fillet, cut into 2 long strips
125g grey mullet, cut into 2 long strips
10g tandoori spices eg turmeric, cumin, coriander
80ml natural yoghurt
1tsp lemon juice
1 bulb fennel
1 large globe artichoke
3 cloves garlic, chopped
50g black olives, chopped
1 small chilli, seeded and chopped
200g small white potatoes
1 bunch basil
1 pinch saffron strands
2 sheets filo pastry
5g cumin seeds
100g lemongrass
5g lime leaves
30g galangal (Thai ginger)
Half a bunch fresh coriander
Half a red onion, chopped
200ml chicken stock
40ml demi-glace
Olive oil
Salt & pepper
A few frisée leaves
Butter

First prepare the tandoori mixture by mixing the tandoori spices with the yoghurt (make your own by keeping full cream milk at 43°C for a few hours), lemon juice, salt and pepper. Marinate the strips of fish overnight in the liquid.

Clean both the fennel and artichoke and cut them into large wedges, then coat them in extra virgin olive oil and grill until tender. Once they have cooled, season with salt and pepper and marinate overnight in extra virgin olive oil with 2 cloves of the garlic, black olives and chilli.

For the basil crushed potatoes boil the potatoes in their skin with sea salt till they are well done. Cut them in half and stir in 50ml of olive oil with the basil, 1 clove of garlic and the saffron. Transfer to a pan with a lid and leave for at least 30 minutes before serving.

Brush one sheet of the filo pastry with melted butter. Drizzle with a few cumin seeds, cover with another layer of pastry and press the two firmly together. Then use a 11cm diameter ring cutter to cut out 8 clean discs. Bake the sheets in the oven at 180°C until golden brown.

In a little olive oil, fry the lemongrass, lime leaves and galangal. Add half the fresh coriander and the chopped red onion. once all the ingredients appear shiny, add the chicken stock and let the mass reduce by two thirds. Add the demi-glace (home made is best) and season to taste. Let the sauce reduce again until it reaches a good thick consistency, then strain.

To finish, warm the fennel and artichoke in a little of the oil marinade and warm up the potatoes and the sauce. Bake the marinated fish, ideally in a tandoori oven: in a tandoor it will require no more than 10 minutes, in an extremely hot (250°C) normal oven slightly longer, but be careful not to overcook. Meanwhile place some of the potatoes, artichokes and fennel in the middle of each plate with a filo disc on top. Remove the fish from the oven and slice into chunks. Arrange one piece each of mullet and salmon with some fennel above the pastry, then another layer of filo. Repeat this whole sequence to create an impressive 'tower'. Ensure it is stable and well layered, then finish decorating with coriander and frisée and drizzle the sauce around the plate.

Black and white sesame crusted mahi-mahi

Maldivian beach lettuce capellini, citrus tomato syrup and vanilla oil

Serves 4

600g mahi-mahi (dorado) fillet

40g butter

150g potatoes

8 leaves dill

800g tomatoes

5g bay leaves

5g oregano

200g capellini

4 yellow cherry tomatoes

4 red cherry tomatoes

500g Maldivian beach lettuce (or young rocket/mizuna)

500g flour

10 eggs

200g fresh okra, large

1 each red, yellow, & green capsicum (about 150g each)

100g sugar

Juice of 3 limes

Juice of 2 oranges

4 sprigs sweet basil

4 sprigs Thai basil

100g black sesame seeds

100g white sesame seeds

20g salt

10g black peppercorn

500ml olive oil

1 vanilla pod

A day in advance halve the vanilla pod, extract the seeds with a knife, and leave to infuse in its skin in 200ml of olive oil.

For the herbed crispy potatoes, first clarify the butter. Peel and cut the potatoes into very thin transparent slices with a mandolin, then prepare an oven tray covered with baking paper. Mix the butter with a little salt and cracked pepper, then lay out a slice of potato and coat with the butter: place a dill leaf in the middle and cover it with another coated potato slice. Make eight in this way, then bake for about 20 minutes at 110°C until the potato is crispy but without colour and set aside.

Blanch four of the tomatoes in boiling water for 1 minute, then immerse in cold water, remove the skins, cut in quarters and take out the seeds. Put the tomato on an oven tray sprinkled with olive oil, salt, and cracked black pepper, then crumble bay leaf and dry oregano over them. Bake for 30 minutes at 100°C. Meanwhile, heat the oil in a deep fat fryer to 180°C then fry the red and yellow cherry tomatoes and a basil sprig for 1 minute; leave on a plate with kitchen paper to absorb the excess oil.

Blanch 400g of the beach lettuce in salted water for 1 minute and quickly cool in cold water. Drain, then blend with one egg to a green paste in a blender. Strain. In a plastic bowl mix the flour, 6 whole eggs, 3 egg yolks, 3g salt and the paste by hand until smooth. Put in the fridge for 30 minutes, then roll out the dough in a pasta machine to a half millimetre thickness. Cut the pasta into thin slices and blanch in salted hot water with a few teaspoons of olive oil for 3 minutes, then drain. Finally, use two forks to lay out the strips on a cool surface to become completely cold.

Remove the seeds from the three capsicums and dice into 7mm cubes. Cook in olive oil in a saucepan over a medium heat for 20 minutes, adding salt, cracked black pepper and the juice of one lime at the end. Blanch the okra for about 6 minutes, making sure it remains a little crunchy, then immerse in cold water to prevent overcooking and reserve.

Mix the sesame seeds on a plate. Season the fish with salt and freshly ground pepper and roll the fillets in the sesame until they are entirely covered. Blanch, peel, quarter, and remove the seeds from the rest of the tomatoes. In a saucepan heat the sugar with the lime and orange juices, then add the chopped tomato and let it cook slowly to a syrup consistency.

When all is ready to serve, heat the fillets in a saucepan with olive oil until the sesame forms a crust on both sides, then bake at 180°C for 5 minutes. While the fish is baking cook the pasta with a few drops of olive oil, salt, and black pepper, and gently reheat the citrus tomato syrup and the sautéd capsicum. Roll the capellini onto the plate with a fork alongside halved fillets; arrange the capsicum with a slice of lime around the centre. With a soup spoon drizzle the citrus tomato syrup and a few drops of vanilla oil, then add the rest of the beach lettuce, a sprig of Thai basil, the fried cherry tomatoes and basil, some fresh dill leaves, and the herbed crispy potato.

SONEVA GILI RESORT & SPA

Lankanfushi Island, North Male Atoll, Maldives

Venison fillet

with chanterelles, potato and herb purée and port sauce

Serves 4

720g venison fillet
300g chanterelles
1 sprig thyme
Olive oil
Butter
Salt & pepper

Port sauce:
125ml port
125ml red Burgundy
200ml court bouillon
125g butter
Salt & pepper

Potato and herb purée:
1kg floury potatoes
50g parsley
10g basil
10g chervil
1 sprig thyme
1 sprig rosemary
100ml milk
100g butter
Nutmeg
Salt & pepper

For the potato and herb purée, boil, peel and mash the potatoes. Add the butter and the milk. Finely chop and add the herbs to the mash: season with salt, pepper and nutmeg.

To prepare the sauce combine the port, red wine and broth in a saucepan and reduce by a third. Beat in the butter and season with salt and pepper. Keep warm.

Season the venison fillet with olive oil, salt and pepper and brown on both sides in olive oil in a heavy frying pan. Add the thyme and roast in the oven at 170°C for about 5 minutes. Leave to rest for 10 minutes. Sweat the chanterelles in butter and season with salt and pepper, then add the thyme leaves and keep warm. Serve as shown.

SPORTHOTEL KRISTIANIA
Lech am Arlberg, Austria

Roselle chicken

Roselle is a flavouring herbal plant grown in Terengganu that contains high levels of vitamin C (ten times that of an orange). The juice – and dried Roselle - is available in specialist food stores.

Serves 2

280g boneless chicken leg, sliced

1 egg

100g Hong Kong flour

30g Bombay onion, cut into wedges

30g green pepper, cut into diamonds

15g spring onion, cut into 5cm lengths

30g fresh roselle

Vegetable oil

Sauce (blend all together):

170ml roselle juice

50g brown sugar

50g chopped tomato

2tsp cognac

Salt

Mix the egg and flour and coat the pieces of sliced chicken with the mixture. Heat the wok and fry the chicken in a little vegetable oil until a light golden brown.

In a separate wok, lightly stir fry the onion and green pepper. Add first the chicken followed by the sauce: toss well until the sauce achieves a syrupy consistency, then add in the spring onions. Serve garnished with Roselle flowers

Green curry fish balls stuffed in rambutan

Serves 2

100g grated mackerel

2 cloves garlic

2 roots coriander

6 rambutan

750ml coconut milk

50g green curry paste (method below)

20g diced aubergine

20g snow peas

30g diced cauliflower

30g diced broccoli

2 ripped kaffir lime leaf

10g sliced red chillies

2g basil leaves

0.5tsp salt

2tsp fish sauce

1tsp palm sugar

Green curry paste:

0.5tsp diced turmeric

2 sticks lemongrass, chopped

3 shallots

20 cloves garlic

2 teaspoons salt

20 hot green chillies

10 chilli peppers

1tsp black peppercorn

1tbs shrimp paste

Pound all the ingredients for the curry paste together until smooth. Add one teaspoon of the curry paste to the mackerel, garlic and coriander and pound until it makes a smooth and sticky fish paste. Add salt to taste.

Peel the rambutan, core out the seed, and stuff the fruit with the fish paste. Bring the coconut milk and curry paste to the boil: add the aubergine, broccoli, cauliflower, snow peas, and kaffir lime leaves, stirring and mixing well. Cook for 2-3 minutes, then add the stuffed rambutan and continue cooking until the fish balls are done. Season with salt, fish sauce and palm sugar to taste. Add basil leaves and the sliced red chillies, continue cooking for a minute, then remove from the heat. Serve hot with steamed rice

TONGSAI GRAND VILLAS
Ko Samui, Surat Thani, Thailand

Filling:

2 duck legs

250g sea salt

50g Chinese five spice

50g crushed black pepper corns

Zest of 1 orange

Zest of one lemon

1 orange & 1 lemon, sliced

Duck fat

5 Bramley apples

50g brown sugar

Dash of Madeira

12 scallops

12 cherry tomatoes

Aged balsamic vinegar

Lettuce and chervil to garnish

Ravioli pasta:

250g of pasta flour

4 egg yolks & 1 whole egg

Saffron water

Salt and pepper

Tomato confit:

7 plum tomatoes, seeded and peeled

3 shallots, finely diced

2 cloves of garlic, chopped

White wine

1 bunch chives, finely chopped

Ravioli of apple and duck confit

with seared scallops and balsamic roast tomatoes

Serves 4

Rub the duck legs with sea salt, peppercorns, five spice, orange and lemon zest and leave in the fridge for 12-24 hours to marinate. Wash the salt and spices off the legs and pat them dry with a clean cloth. Place into the melted duck fat with the slices of orange and lemon and cook slowly for 3 hours at 120°C.

Whilst the duck legs are cooking, make up the ravioli pasta by placing all the ingredients, apart from the saffron water, into a food processor bowl. Start to mix together then add the saffron water until the mixture begins to come together. Remove and make into a smooth ball with your hands, then wrap in cling film and leave to rest for at least half an hour. Meanwhile, sauté the shallots and garlic with a little butter, then add the chopped tomatoes, cook for 1-2 minutes, then add a splash of white wine and cook until the liquid has condensed. Leave to cool slightly and add the chopped chives.

When the duck legs are cooked let them cool slightly then break off the meat from the bones, discarding any fat and gristle. Chop the duck meat and add a little Madeira to taste, re-adjust the seasoning if necessary, and leave to one side. Peel and chop the apples into 2cm dice. Sauté the apples in a little butter and brown sugar until al dente, then mix the apples into the duck mix.

To make up the ravioli, roll out the pasta – setting number 6 on a pasta machine– onto a floured surface. Cut the sheet into 8 squares with sides of around 6cm, place a generous amount of filling in the centre of four of the squares (the bottom layers) and use an egg wash to stick down the top layers; make sure there are no air bubbles. Cut out with a fluted round cutter and set aside.

For the balsamic roasted tomatoes, heat the oven to 200°C. Bring the tomatoes to the boil in an oven-proof pan with the balsamic vinegar, salt and pepper, then transfer to the oven for 5 minutes. Meanwhile, heat a non-stick frying pan for the scallops. Season the scallops with salt and pepper, and add to the pan with a little oil and butter. Cook for 1 minute on each side and finish with a squeeze of lemon juice.

To serve, blanch the ravioli in boiling salted water for 2-3 minutes. Spoon out a little of the warm tomato confit with the ravioli on top. Arrange the scallops, (3 per person) and tomatoes around the ravioli and finish with balsamic vinegar and sprigs of chervil.

TYLNEY HALL

Rotherwick, Hook, Hampshire, UK

Olive crusted rack of lamb

with preserved lemon jus

serves 4

1.2kg rack of lamb
40g fresh bread crumbs
60g chopped black Kalamata olives
40g chopped green olives
12g mixed herbs
40ml extra virgin olive oil
20g Dijon mustard
8g salt
12g crushed black pepper

Sauce:

100g lemon
8g salt
5g Cayenne pepper
40g sugar
50g shallots
1 sprig thyme
50ml port
500ml lamb stock
40g butter

Garlic mash:

400g potatoes
150ml cream
15g finely chopped garlic
40g butter
4g ground nutmeg
5g salt
3g ground white pepper

To begin preparation for the sauce, cut each lemon into 8 pieces and remove the seeds. Apply salt and Cayenne pepper and sprinkle with sugar, then dry the wedges in the oven at 50°C for 2 hours.

Sauté the shallots in a little of the butter, add the thyme and deglaze the pan with the port. Add the lamb stock and reduce to a thick sauce consistency. Strain the sauce through a fine strainer into a pan, add the lemon confit and simmer for a few minutes to allow the flavour to infuse. Finish by swirling in cold cubes of butter and seasoning.

Peel and boil the potatoes. In a separate pan, combine the cream, garlic and butter and keep aside. Pass the boiled potatoes through a food mill to get a fine paste, then add the cream and butter emulsion to the mashed potatoes. Blend with a wooden spoon until smooth and fluffy and season to taste.

Season the lamb rack with a little extra virgin olive oil. Prepare the crust by mixing together the breadcrumbs, chopped olives, mixed herbs and olive oil. Sear the lamb rack in a pan on a high heat, then smear the meat with the Dijon mustard and coat with the crust. Roast the lamb in a pre-heated oven at 180°C until it is pink – about 15 minutes.

To serve, spoon the mashed potatoes on the plate and arrange vegetables of your choice, blanched and tossed in butter. Cut the lamb into two cutlets with the sauce poured around: shown here garnished with garlic confit and a sprig of thyme.

THE OBEROI UDAIVILAS, UDAIPUR

Udaipur, India

Quail curry

Serves 4

8 whole quail, de-skinned

Marinade:

20g Red Kashmiri chilli powder

1tsp turmeric powder

50g freshly made ginger and garlic paste

1g saffron soaked in water

Juice of 1 lemon

Salt to taste

Curry sauce:

75ml sunflower oil

6 green cardamom pods

150g onion, finely sliced

1tsp coriander powder

0.5tsp whole black peppercorn

150g fresh tomato purée

100g whisked yoghurt

50ml clarified butter

20 sprigs chopped fresh coriander

Juice of 1 lemon

Mix the marinating ingredients to a paste and smear over the quail. Cover and leave to infuse for 6 hours.

Heat the oven to 180°C. Transfer the quail to a roasting tray, and surround them with the marinade. Roast for 15 minutes until the quail is semi-cooked.

Prepare the curry sauce by heating the sunflower oil in a heavy bottomed casserole. Add the green cardamom and the thinly sliced onions and cook until the onions turn golden. Add the coriander powder and peppercorns. Stir for 3-4 minutes then add the fresh tomato purée and the whisked yoghurt. Simmer for 15 to 20 minutes, add salt and stir, then pass the curry through a strainer into a heavy bottomed pan and set aside.

To finish, add the semi-cooked quail to the strained gravy and cook for another 10 minutes. Check the seasoning and add the ghee or clarified butter, coriander, and lemon juice. Serve hot accompanied by steamed rice and buttered naan bread

THE OBEROI VANYAVILAS, RANTHAMBHORE

Sawai Madhopur, Rajasthan, India

Beetroot with Roccaverano soft cheese

lettuce, pine-seed and raisin gazpacho

Serves 4

2 beetroot

200g Roccaverano cheese

4 lettuce hearts, thinly sliced

1 fresh onion

10g pine-seeds

25g raisins

Juice of half a lemon

Extra virgin olive oil

Salt & pepper

Bake the beetroot for an hour in a medium oven, then allow to cool and remove the peel. Make a thick paste by combining the soft cheese with a little extra virgin olive oil and salt to taste. Cut each beetroot into 6 round slices: build four millefeuille using three slices sandwiching the cheese mixture.

Cut the onion into a julienne and sauté in a little oil until lightly browned. Add the lettuce, pine-seeds, raisins and lemon juice, then continue cooking over a low heat for a further 5 minutes. Leave to cool, then transfer to a processor and blend to a soft cream.

Corona de Robala relleno con morillas

Baked white sea bass stuffed with morels

Serves 4

4x 150g fillets white sea bass (robalo)

Juice of half a lime

2tbs mayonnaise

150ml pesto

400g (2) potatoes

50g Parmesan cheese

For the duxelle:

100g morel mushrooms

25g bacon

Half an onion

25ml double cream

15g Parmesan

For the sauce:

Half an onion chopped

2 garlic cloves, chopped

20g tomato paste

1 cup tomato juice

500g tomatoes, cut into small cubes

10g basil leaves

Butter

Olive oil

Salt & pepper

4 circular 10cm moulds

Marinate the fish fillets in the lime juice, mayonnaise, pesto and salt and pepper for 2 hours. Meanwhile, prepare the duxelle by pan frying the morel mushrooms, bacon, garlic and onion, all finely chopped, in a little olive oil. Add the cream and Parmesan, season with salt and set aside.

To prepare the sauce, sauté the onion and garlic in olive oil and butter until lightly browned, then add the tomato paste and simmer for 5 minutes. Add the tomato juice, the tomato cubes, and the basil leaves, then continue to simmer until the liquid reduces to a thick sauce consistency. Season with salt and pepper and keep warm.

Boil and cut the potatoes into slices, then sauté in butter and olive oil; season with salt and pepper. Position each marinated fish fillet around the inside of a mould, then fill the empty centre with the sautéd potato slices and duxelle; top with Parmesan cheese. Cook in the oven at 180°C for 15 minutes

Remove from the mould and arrange on a plate. Decorate with a rosette of potato purée with chopped black olives, add the sauce around the plate.

Shown with a garnish of deep fried aubergine chips, with potato and chopped olive purée, sautéd potato slices and green fava beans around the plate.

HOTEL VILLA MONTANA

Morelia, Mich, Mexico

Calamar de Potera filled with boletus and chicharrones with green pea purée

Chicharrones are a local wild boar sausage

Serves 6

3 x 25cm lengths of squid

250g peas

200g boletus

200g chicharrones
(or other wild boar sausage)

1 onion

4 tomatoes

100ml extra virgin olive oil

Maldon sea salt

1 cooking bag

The timing of the various cooking processes in this recipe is critical.

First peel and lightly fry the onion and tomatoes over a low heat. Meanwhile, clean the boletus with a small brush, cut them into julienne and sauté in a few drops of olive oil.

Slice the chicharrones very finely – preferably in a cold slicer: reserve 3 slices, finely chopping the remainder. When the tomatoes and onions are ready, add the seasoned boletus and chopped sausages. Clean the squid both inside and out with cold water, being careful not to break the tubes, then fill them with the mixture. Put the filled tubes into the bag and cook them in a vapour oven at 90°C for 2 hours, then cool the bag with iced water.

Blanch and refresh the peas, then blitz them in a processor, adding salt and olive oil to achieve a smooth purée. Halve the 3 slices of chicharrones previously set aside and dry them out in a low oven between two pieces of blotting paper until they are crisp.

To serve, reheat the squid in a frying pan over a low heat. Accompany with the cream of peas and crisped chicarrones on top: decorate with a ribbon of extra virgin olive oil and a few crystals of Maldon salt.

VILLA REAL

Madrid, Spain

A rich selection of seafood

with a touch of white wine, olive oil, butter and herbs

For each person:

40g fillet of red snapper or other firm-fleshed fish

50g lobster

60g crayfish

60g small shrimp

25g green mussels

20g tiger shrimp

25g octopus, precooked

10g parsley, chopped

40ml extra virgin olive oil

15ml white wine

20ml fish stock

Juice of half a lemon

20g butter

Salt & pepper to taste

Mix all the dry ingredients together in a pan. Pour over the oil, wine, stock, and lemon juice, add the butter, and cover the pan with foil. Cook in the oven at 180°C for 20 minutes.

Serve with sautéed vegetables and mashed potatoes, decorated with a rose of tomato and a sprig of parsley.

VILLA ROLANDI GOURMET & BEACH CLUB

Isla Mujeres, Mexico

Pan seared guinea fowl

on flash fried mushrooms accompanied by a creamy polenta, topped with a vegetable and guinea fowl sausage and complimented by a chardonnay jus

Serves 2

THE VILLAGE AT SPIER

Stellenbosch, South Africa

1 whole guinea fowl
(breasts are about 140g each)

Polenta:

90g polenta

8g onion

2g garlic

2g thyme

15ml cream

10ml butter

Salt & ground pepper

Sausage:

1 egg white

30ml cream

8g broccoli

8g red peppers

8g corn

8g yellow peppers

30cm sausage skin

Jus:

180ml guinea fowl stock (used for the finished jus)

Guinea fowl bones

Tomato paste

250ml red wine

Mirepoix

500ml chardonnay

40g assorted mushrooms (dried and rehydrated)

10 ml clarified butter

30g spinach

10g diced onions

20ml cream

Debone the fowl and take the two breasts with the leg joint still attached (suprême). Remove all possible meat from the bird to use in the sausage.

To prepare the jus, make a dark stock from the guinea fowl by roasting off the bones in the oven. Dice the vegetables for a mirepoix and roast in a tilting pan; add the tomato purée and roast further, adding the bones to the tilting pan. Deglaze the pan 3 times with red wine, then add water and slowly reduce for 12 hours, topping up the liquid from time to time. Finally, reduce the chardonnay in a saucepan, add the guinea fowl stock and continue reducing to a thickened jus: you should end up with 100ml of sauce for the two servings. Finish with a little cream.

For the sausage, blend the meat from the bird, adding the egg white, seasoning and cream. Sauté the vegetables and add to the farce mixture. Transfer the mixture to a piping bag and pipe out into the sausage skin. Preheaat the oven to 180°C: divide the sausage in two, pan sear to colour the outside, then finish with 6-8 minutes in the oven.

To prepare the polenta, sauté off the onion, garlic, thyme and add the polenta and stock or water. Season and add the cream.

When ready to serve, season and pan fry the guinea fowl breasts in clarified butter and place under a salamander or grill to finish cooking. Pan fry the assorted mushrooms in butter, adding seasoning. Sauté off the onions, add the cream and toss in the spinach: season. Assemble the plate as shown.

Lavender honey glazed lamb

with blueberry gastrique

Serves 4

2 x 350g lamb racks

250ml honey

2tbs dried lavender

1.5 cups cooked Yellow Stone ground grits

100g aged white cheddar, grated

100g courgette, diced

100g yellow squash, diced

1tbs butter

Honeycomb & lavender bloom for garnish

Kosher salt & cracked black pepper

Blueberry gastrique:

1.5 litres Merlot

1 litre frozen blueberries

375ml red wine vinegar

125ml honey

Half cup herbes de Provence

2 pints of fresh blueberries, halved

For the blueberry compote, combine all the ingredients except the fresh berries in a saucepan and simmer until reduced by two thirds. Strain through a fine mesh strainer, chill, then add the fresh blueberries. Reserve for use.

Preheat the oven to 200°C. Season the lamb with salt and pepper and set aside. Gently warm the honey and lavender in a small saucepan over a low flame for about 10 minutes. Combine the white cheddar with the cooked grits and keep warm.

Sear the lamb rack fat side down in a hot pan and brown on each side. Brush the honey over the lamb and transfer to the oven for 10-15 minutes for medium rare. Sauté the courgettes and squash in the butter and season to taste.

To serve, arrange half the grits in the centre of the plate and drizzle the blueberry gastrique around. Slice the lamb and fan on top of the grits. Add the squashes to either side of the lamb and garnish with honeycomb and lavender bloom.

CIRCA 1886 AT WENTWORTH MANSION ®

Charleston, South Carolina, USA

Smoked trout hash

with Yukon potatoes, Poblano peppers and sunny up quail egg

Serves 4

WHITEHALL HOTEL

Chicago, Illinois, USA

300g smoked trout, de-boned & broken into bite-sized pieces

1kg Yukon gold potatoes, skinned & steamed

1 red pepper

1 yellow pepper

2 shallots, peeled & diced

1tbs fine herbs (equal parts tarragon, parsley, chives, thyme & chervil)

4 quail eggs

3tbs butter

1 Poblano chilli pepper

Kosher salt & fresh cracked black pepper to taste

Begin by dicing the cooked Yukon potatoes into 1cm cubes. Finely dice the peppers into brunoise size (5mm) pieces. Chop and combine all of the fresh herbs

Melt 2 tablespoons of butter in a large, medium-heated skillet then sauté the shallots and diced peppers until soft. Next, add the potatoes and toss the ingredients to combine. Let the hash sit for 2 to 3 minutes on one side to allow potatoes to brown. Toss again and add the trout. Allow the hash to sit again for 2 to 3 minutes to brown the other sides of the potato.

Melt the remaining tablespoon of butter in another non-stick, pan. Break the quail eggs into the pan, being careful to keep them apart. Season with salt and pepper and cook until the eggs are sunny up.

Divide the hash onto 4 warm serving plates, piling it high in the middle of the plate with an egg on top. Garnish with whole fresh herbs and roasted Poblano hollandaise. Serve immediately.

A composition of fish

Serves 5

10 scallops

20 tiger prawns

15 mussels

15 clams

500g red snapper

300g baby spinach

2 leeks

1 bulb fennel

300g butter

1 bunch coriander

Fumet de poisson:

1 stalk of celery

2 onions

1 carrot

1 bulb fennel

1 Jalapeño pepper

1tbs of grape seed oil

2tbs butter

6 cloves garlic, crushed

3 kg bones from lean fish ie flounder/sole/halibut

750ml dry white wine

3 litres cold water

Bouquet garni

The fumet de poisson is the highly flavoured fish stock in which the clams and mussels will cook, and can be prepared well in advance. Begin by dicing the celery, onions, carrots pepper and fennel, then sauté them in the grape seed oil and butter in a large pan until translucent. Add the garlic, then the fish bones. Stir the ingredients over medium heat for a couple of minutes, then deglaze with the white wine and add the water. Gently bring the stock to simmer, and add the bouquet garni. Skim off any fat or scum, simmer for 40 minutes, then strain.

Return the strained stock to the heat and bring to a simmer. Slice the leeks and add them to the stock with the clams; after another 3 minutes add the mussels and let the pan simmer for a further 40-60 minutes. Lightly sauté the spinach and fennel in butter. In a separate pan sauté the red snapper in butter on a medium heat, then after 2 minutes add the scallops, cooking for one minute on one side only. Serve as shown, garnishing with coriander leaves.

WINDSOR ARMS HOTEL

Toronto, Ontario, Canada

New England lobster and crab cakes

with smoked corn slaw and spicy remoulade

Serves 4

250g fresh lobster meat

250g lump crab meat

1 cup fresh breadcrumbs (plus extra for coating)

2tbs yellow pepper, small dice

2tbs red pepper, small dice

2tbs red onion, small dice

1tsp chopped fresh garlic

250ml mayonnaise

2tbs fresh lemon juice

2tbs chopped capers

Salt & freshly ground black pepper

Old Bay seasoning

Worcestershire sauce

Tabasco sauce

Extra virgin olive oil

Remoulade:

125ml mayonnaise

1tbs red onion, small dice

1tsp fresh garlic, finely minced

2tbs chopped cornichons

1tbs chopped capers

1tbs fresh lemon juice

1tbs yellow pepper, small dice

1tbs red pepper, small dice

Cayenne pepper

Tabasco

Salt & freshly ground black pepper

Smoked corn slaw:

1 cup sliced green cabbage

1/4 cup smoked corn

1/4 cup carrot, julienne

125ml mayonnaise

50ml red wine vinegar

15ml fresh lemon juice

2tbs sugar

1/4 cup yellow pepper, julienne

1/4 cup red pepper, julienne

Salt & freshly ground white pepper

Lightly sauté the garlic, shallots and peppers in olive oil. Put the lobster and crab meat in a large bowl and add the sautéed aromatics and the capers. Add the breadcrumbs by hand, and carefully combine so as not to break up the crab and lobster. When fully incorporated, carefully add the mayonnaise and lemon juice to achieve a firm but moist consistency that will hold its shape when sautéed. Finish by seasoning to taste with salt, pepper, Tabasco, Old Bay and Worcestershire sauces, then shape 12 cakes out of the mix. Lightly coat each cake with breadcrumbs and sauté in clarified butter until golden brown.

To prepare the remoulade, thoroughly mix all the ingredients in a bowl. Season well; it should be a classic remoulade with a bite.

For the corn slaw, whisk together the vinegar, sugar and mayonnaise then fold in all the remaining ingredients and combine thoroughly. Season to taste, then let rest for 15 minutes.

To serve, place a good dessert spoonful of remoulade on a warm plate. Place a heaping spoon of slaw on the plate with crab cakes alongside. Garnish with smoked corn, sliced chives and brumoise of pepper.

CONVERSION TABLES

OVEN TEMPERATURES

°celcius	**70**	**100**	**120**	**140**	**160**	**170**	**180**	**190**	**200**	**210**	**220**	**230**	**240**
°fahrenheit	160	215	250	285	320	340	355	375	395	410	430	450	475
gas (regulo)	0	1/4	1/2	1	3	4	4	5	6	6	7	8	9

GRAMS - OUNCES

Divide g by 28.35

Table below is rounded up or down for convenience

g	**5**	**10**	**25**	**50**	**75**	**100**	**125**	**150**	**200**	**250**	**500**	**750**	**Kilo**
oz	0.2	0.5	1	1.75	2.5	3.5	4.5	5	7	9	17.5	26.5	35

MILLILITRES - FLUID OUNCES

Divide ml by 29.57

Table below is rounded up or down for convenience

ml	**5**	**10**	**25**	**50**	**75**	**100**	**125**	**150**	**200**	**250**	**500**	**750**	**Litre**
fl oz	0.2	0.5	1	1.75	2.5	3.5	4.25	5	7	8.5	17	25	34

CENTIMETRES - INCHES

Divide cm by 2.54

INDEX OF RECIPES

H-K

L

M-N

O-P

Q-R

S

T

V-W

HOTEL INFORMATION

AFRICA & INDIAN OCEAN	CHEF	PAGE
Kenya BATELEUR CAMP AT KICHWA TEMBO Private Bag X27, Benmore 2010, South Africa T:0027 118094300 F: 0027 118094400 E: information@ccarfica.com www.ccafrica.com	George Musembi	18
Mauritius THE OBEROI, MAURITIUS Turtle Bay, Pointe Aux Piments, Mauritius T: 00230 204 3600 F: 00230 204 3625 E: reservations@oberoi-mauritius.com www.oberoihotels.com	Andrew Skinner	108
South Africa EKLAND SAFARIS PO Box 3187, Louis Trichardt 0920, South Africa T: 00 3491 6585220 F: 00 3491 6585251 E: yawankayali@eklandsafaris.com www.eklandsafaris.com	Janneman L Lee	56
NGALA PRIVATE GAME RESERVE Private Bag X27, Benmore 2010, South Africa T: 0027 11 8094300 F: 0027 11 8094400 E: information@ccarfica.com www.ccafrica.com	Dumi Elmon Ndlovu	102
THE VILLAGE AT SPIER R310 Lyneroch Road, Stellenbosch, South Africa T: 0027 21 8091166 F: 0027 21 8091136 E: info@spier.co.za www.spier.co.za	Craig Cormack	154

AMERICAS & THE CARIBBEAN		
Barbados CORAL REEF CLUB St James, Barbados, West Indies T: 001 246 422 2372 F: 001 246 422 1776 E: coral@caribsurf.com www.coralreefbarbados.com	Graham Licorish	40
Canada WINDSOR ARMS HOTEL 18 St Thomas Street, Toronto, Ontario M5S 3E7, Canada T: 001 416 971 9666 F: 001 416 921 9121 E: reserve@windsorarmshotel.com www.windsorarmshotel.com	Alexander Austriaco	160
Costa Rica HOTEL PUNTA ISLITA Guanacaste, Costa Rica T: 00506 290 4259 F: 00506 232 2183 E: marketingdir@hotelpuntaislita.com www.hotelpuntaislita.com	Lissette Viales	116

AMERICAS & THE CARIBBEAN continued	CHEF	PAGE
USA continued		
HOTEL PARISI & LE TAPENADE 1111 Prospect Street, La Jolla, CA 92037, USA T: 001 858 454 1511 F: 001 858 454 1531 E: info@hotelparisi.com www.hotelparisi.com	Jean-Michele Diot	112
MONMOUTH PLANTATION 36 Melrose Avenue, Natchez, Mississippi 39120, USA T: 001 601 442 5852 F: 001 601 446 7762 E: luxury@monmouthplantation.com www.monmouthplantation.com	Lanny Brasher	100
POST RANCH INN Post Office Box 219, Big Sur, CA 93920, USA T: 001 831 667 2200 F: 001 831 667 2824 E: dan@postranchinn.com www.postranchinn.com	Craig von Foerster	114
THE INN AT MONTCHANIN VILLAGE PO Box 130, Rte 100, Kirk Road, Montchanin, DE 19710, USA T: 001 302 888 2133 F: 001 302 888 0389 E: inn@montchanin.com www.montchanin.com	Todd Snyder	78
THE INN AT SOUTHBRIDGE 1020 Main Street, St Helena, CA 94574, USA T: 001 707 967 9400 F: 001 707 967 9486 E: jwhitehead@meadowood.com www.innatsouthbridge.com	Michael Reardon	80
WENTWORTH MANSION 149 Wentworth Street, Charleston, SC 29401, USA T: 001 843 722 8680 F: 001 843 722 8634 E: melissa@charminginns.com www.wentworthmansion.com	Marc Collins	156
THE WHITEHALL HOTEL 105 East Delaware DL, Chicago, IL 60611 , USA T: 001 312 944 6300 F: 001 312 573 6205 E: info@thewhitehallhotel.com www.thewhitehallhotel.com	Joseph Rosetti	158
WOODSTOCK INN AND RESORT 14 The Green, Woodstock, VT 05091- 1298, USA T: 001 802 457 1100 F: 001 802 457 6699 E: email@woodstockinn.com www.woodstockinn.com	Daniel Jackson	162

ASIA & PACIFIC	CHEF	PAGE
Australia		
LAKE HOUSE		
Kings Street, Daylesford, 3460, Australia		
T: 0061 3 53483329 F: 0061 3 53483995		
E: enquiries@lakehouse.com.au www.lakehouse.com.au	Alla Wolf- Tasker	88
Fiji		
NUKUBATI ISLAND		
PO Box 1928, Labasa, Fiji Islands		
T: 0061 2 93888196 F: 0061 2 93888204		
E: info@nukubati.com www.nukubati.com	Ms Taraivini Marama	104
India		
KUMARAKOM LAKE RESORT		
Kumarakom North, Kottayam, Kerala, India - 686566		
T: 0091 481 2524900 F: 0091 481 2524987		
E: klresort@vsnl.com www.klresort.com	Swapan Kumar Baidya	86
THE OBEROI AMARVILAS, AGRA		
Taj East Gate, Agra 282 001, Uttar Pradesh, India		
T: 0091 562 2231515 F: 0091 562 2231516		
E: gm@oberoi-amarvilas.com www.oberoihotels.com	Siddharth Chowhry	8
THE OBEROI RAJVILAS, JAIPUR		
Goner Road, Jaipur 303 012, Rajasthan, India		
T: 0091 141 2680101 F: 0091 141 2680202		
E: gm@oberoi-rajvilas.com www.oberoihotels.com	Andrew Whiffen	122
THE OBEROI UDAIVILAS, UDAIPUR		
Haridasji Ki Magri, Udaipur 313 001, India		
T: 0091 294 243 3300 F: 0091 294 243 3200		
E: gm@oberoi-udaivilas.com www.oberoihotels.com	Jean Christophe Basseau	142
THE OBEROI VANYAVILAS, RANTHAMBHORE		
Ranthambore Road, Sawai Madhopur 322 001, Rajasthan, India		
T: 0091 7462 23999 F: 0091 7462 23988		
E: gm@oberoi-vanyavilas.com www.oberoihotels.com		144
Indonesia		
THE OBEROI, BALI		
Seminyak Beach, Jalan Laksmana, PO Box 3351, Denpasar 80033, Bali, Indonesia		
T: 0062 361 730 361 F: 0062 361 730 791		
E: mhagenbach@theoberoi-bali.com www.oberoihotels.com	Mark Hagenbach	106
PURI WULANDARI: A BOUTIQUE RESORT AND SPA		
Kedewatan, Ubud - Gianyar, Bali, Indonesia		
T: 0062 361 980 252 F: 0062 361 980 253		
E: dnucira@cbn.net.id www.puriwulandari.net	Dharmen Makawana	118

ASIA & PACIFIC continued	CHEF	PAGE
Malaysia		
PANGKOR LAUT ISLAND Pangkor Laut Island, 32200 Lumut, Perak, Malaysia T: 0060 (0)5 6991100 F: 60 (0)5 6991200 E: lmyter@ytlhotels.com.my www.pangkorlautresort.com	Wai Look Chow	110
TANJONG JARA RESORT Batu 8 off Jalan Dungun, 23000 Dungun, Malaysia T: 00 609 845 1100 F: 00 609 845 6014 E: tjara@po.jaring.my www.tanjongjararesort.com	Lim Chua Seng	136
Maldives		
SONEVA FUSHI RESORT & SPA Kunfunadhoo Island, Baa Atoll, Maldives T: 00 960 230304 F: 00 960 230335 E: clm@sixsenses.com www.sixsenses.com	Remon Alphenaar	130
SONEVA GILI RESORT & SPA Lankanfushi Island, North Male Atoll, Maldives T: 00 960 230304 F: 00 960 230335 E: clm@sixsenses.com www.sixsenses.com/sonevagili	Lional Valla	132
New Zealand		
BLANKET BAY Glenorchy, New Zealand T: 00 64 3 4429442 F: 00 64 3 4429441 E: pjenkins@blanketbay.com www.blanketbay.com	Jason Dell	22
EICHARDT'S PRIVATE HOTEL PO Box 1340, Marine Parade, Queenstown, New Zealand T: 00 64 3 441 0450 F: 00 64 3 441 0440 E: stay@eichardtshotel.co.nz www.eichardts.co.nz	Alan Chrastecky	54
HUKA LODGE Huka Falls Rd, PO Box 95, Taupo, New Zealand T: 00 64 7 378 5791 F: 00 64 7 378 0427 E: reservations@hukalodge.co.nz www.hukalodge.com	Nicholas Watt	76
THE GEORGE CHRISTCHURCH PO Box 13063, Christchurch, New Zealand T: 00 64 33710254 F: 00 64 33666747 E: pa@thegeorge.com www.thegeorge.com	Hamish Brown	60
Sri Lanka		
LIGHTHOUSE HOTEL & SPA Dadella, Galle, Sri Lanka T: 00 94 9 2224017 F: 00 94 9 2224021 E: lighthouse@lighthouse.lk www.jetwinghotels.com	Nihal Senanayake	92

	Chef	Page
SAMAN VILLAS Aturuwella, Bentota, Sri Lanka T: 00 94 34 2275435 F: 00 94 34 2275433 E: samanvil@sri.lanka.net www.samanvilla.com	Athula Abeygunawardana	128
Thailand		
BANYAN TREE BANGKOK 211 Upper Bukit Timah Road, Singapore 588182, Singapore T: 00 65 6849 5892 F: 00 65 6462 3800 E: maisy.koh@banyantree.com www.banyantree.com	Ian Sherlock	16
TONGSAI GRAND VILLAS 84 Moo 5, Bophut, Ko Samui, Surat Thani 84320, Thailand T: 00 66 77 245544 F: 00 66 77 425462 E: info@tongsaibay.co.th www.tongsaibay.co.th	Prapai Chuanit	138

EUROPE

	Chef	Page
Austria		
SPORTHOTEL KRISTIANIA Omesberg 331, Lech am Arlberg 6764, Austria T: 00 43 5583 25610 F: 00 43 5583 3550 E: kristiania@lech.at www.kristiania.at	Richard Brunnauer	134
Belgium		
DIE SWAENE Steenhouwersdijk 1, B -8000 Bruges, Belgium T: 00 32 50 342 798 F. 00 32 50 336 674 E: info@dieswaene.hotel.com www.dieswaene-hotel.com	Peter De Pauw	48
Channel Islands		
THE ATLANTIC HOTEL Le Mont de la Pulente, St Brelade, Jersey, JE3 8HE T: 00 44 (0)1534 744101 F: 00 44(0)1534 744102 E: info@theatlantichotel.com www.theatlantichotel.com	Ken Healy	12
Cyprus		
THE CLASSIC HOTEL 94 Rigenis Street, PO Box 21758, 1513 Nicosia, Cyprus T: 00 357 22 664006 F: 00 357 22 670072 E: classic@gapgroup.com www.classic.com.cy	Dimitris Ioannou	38
England		
ASHDOWN PARK HOTEL & COUNTRY CLUB Wych Cross, Near Forest Row, East Sussex, RH18 5JR T: 00 44 (0)1342 824988 F: 00 44 (0)1342 826206 E: reservations@ashdownpark.com www.ashdownpark.com	John McManus	10

EUROPE continued	CHEF	PAGE
DANESFIELD HOUSE HOTEL & SPA Henley Road, Marlow, Bucks, SL7 2EY T: 00 44 (0)1628 891010 F: 00 44 (0)1628 890408 E: sales@danesfieldhouse.co.uk www.danesfieldhouse.co.uk	Damian Broom	46
DORSET SQUARE HOTEL 39 Dorset Square, London, NW1 6QN T: 00 44 (0)207 723 7874 F: 00 44 (0)207 724 3328 E: gm@dorsetsquare.co.uk www.dorsetsquare.co.uk	John Woodward	50
THE CHESTER GROSVENOR & GROSVENOR SPA Eastgate, Chester, CH1 1LT T: 00 44 (0)1244 324024 F: 00 44 (0)1244 313246 E: chesgrov@chestergrosvenor.com www.chestergrosvenor.com	Simon Radley	34
THE GRAND HOTEL King Edwards Parade, Eastbourne, East Sussex, BN21 4EQ T: 00 44 (0)1323 412345 F: 00 44 (0)1323 412233 E: reservations@grandeastbourne.com www.grandeastbourne.com	Gerald Röser	64
TYLNEY HALL Rotherwick, Hook, Hampshire, RG27 9AZ T: 00 44 (0)1256 764 881 F: 00 44 (0)1256 768141 E: reservations@tylneyhall.com www.tylneyhall.com	Stephen Hine	140
France		
CHÂTEAU EZA Rue De La Pise, F-06360, Eze Village, France T: 00 33 (0)493 411224 F: 00 33 (0)493 411664 E: info@chateaueza.com www.chateaueza.com	Christophe L'Hospitalier	28
CHATEAU LA CHENEVIERE Escures-Commes, 14520 Port-en-Bessin, Normandy, France T: 00 33 (0)2 3151 25 25 F: 00 33 (0)2 31 51 25 20 E: la.cheneviere@wanadoo.fr www.lacheneviere.com	Claude Esprabens	32
HOTEL CHATEAU GRAND BARRAIL Route de Libourne, 33330 Saint-Emilion, France T: 00 33 (0)557 553700 F: 00 33 (0)557 553749 E: welcome@grand-barrail.com www.grand-barrail.com	Fabrice Giraud	30
LE MANOIR DE BELLERIVE Rout de Siorac, 24480, Le Buisson de Cadouin, France T: 00 33 (0)553 221616 F: 00 33 (0)553 22 0905 E: manoir.bellerive@wanadoo.fr www.bellerirehotel.com	Eric Barbe	90

HOTEL INFORMATION

	CHEF	PAGE
Greece		
AEGEAN SUITES HOTEL Megali Ammos, Skiathos Island, 37002 Skiathos, Greece T: 00 30 2 4270 24066 F: 00 30 2 4270 24070 E: suites@otenet.gr www.aegeansuites.com	Malis Savas	6
EAGLES PALACE 63075, Ouranouplis, Halkidiki, Greece T: 00 30 237 703 1101 F: 00 30 237 703 1383 E: eaglespl@otenet.gr www.eaglespalace.gr	Iordanis Leonidas	52
KATIKIES 84702 Oia, Santorini, Greece T: 00 30 228 607 1401 F: 00 30 228 6071129 E: katikies@otenet.gr www.katikies.com	Ilias Taousanis	82
MINOS BEACH ART'OTEL Aghios Nikolaos, 72100 Crete, Greece T: 00 30 28410 22345-9 F: 00 30 28410 22548 E: info-minos@bluegr.com www.bluegr.com	Michael Zehry	98
RODOS PARK SUITES HOTEL 12 Riga Fereou Str, 85100 Rodos, Greece T: 00 30 22410 89700 F: 00 30 22410 24613 E: info@rodospark.gr www.rodospark.gr	George Paleologos	126
Italy		
GRAND HOTEL MAJESTIC Via Vittorio Veneto, 32, Verbania Pallanza, I - 28922, Piedmont, Italy T: 00 39 (0)323 504305 F: 00 39 (0)323 556379 E: sales@grandhotelmajestic.it www.grandhotelmajestic.it	Giuseppe Saglio	66
GROTTA GIUSTI SPA HOTEL Via Grotta Giusti 1411, 51015 Monsummano Terme, Pistoia, Italy T: 00 39 0572 90771 F: 00 39 0572 9077200 E: info@grottagiustispa.com www.grottagiustispa.com	Giuseppe Argentino	70
HOTEL VILLA CRESPI Via Fava 18, 28016 Orta San Guillo, Italy T: 00 39 0322 911902 F: 00 39 0322 911919 E: villacrespi@lagodortahotels.com www.lagodortahotels.com	Antonino Cannavacciuolo	146
LONDRA PALACE Riva degli Schiavoni 4171, 30122 Venice, Italy T: 00 39 041 5200533 F: 00 39 041 5225032 E: info@hotelondra.it www.hotelondra.it	Mr Stefano Mazzone	94

EUROPE continued	CHEF	PAGE
The Netherlands BLAKES AMSTERDAM Keizersgracht 384, 1016 GB, Amsterdam, The Netherlands T: 0031 (0)20 5302010 F: 00 31 (0)20 5302030 E: hotel@blakes.nl www.blakesamsterdam.com	Schilo Van Coevoorden	20
Portugal QUINTA DA CASA BRANCA Rua Da Casa Branca 7, 9000-088 Funchal, Portugal T: 00 351 291 700770 F: 00 351 291 765070 E: estalagem@quintacasabranca.pt www.quintacasabranca.pt	Vitor Sobral	120
Scotland BALBIRNIE HOUSE Balbirnie Park, Markinch, Fife KY7 6NE, Scotland T: 00 44 (0)1592 610066 F: 00 44 (0)1592 610529 E: info@balbirnie.co.uk www.balbirnie.co.uk	Ian MacDonald	14
THE MARCLIFFE AT PITFODELS North Deeside Road, Aberdeen, AB15 9YA, Scotland T: 00 44 (0)1224 861000 F: 00 44 (0)1224 868860 E: enquiries@marcliffe.com www.marcliffe.com	Michael Stoddart	96
Spain HOTEL CLARIS Pau Claris 150, 08009, Spain T: 00 34 934876262 F: 00 34 932 157970 E: claris@derbyhotels.es www.derbyhotels.es	Miquel Calzado	36
VILLA REAL Plaza De Las Cortes 10, 28014, Madrid, Spain T: 00 34 914203767 F: 0034 914202547 E: villareal@derbyhotels.es www.derbyhotels.es	Joaquin Felipe	150
Switzerland GRAND HOTEL VILLA CASTAGNOLA Viale Castagnola 31, 6906 Lugano, Switzerland T: 00 41 91 973 25 55 F: 00 41 91 973 25 50 E: info@villa-castagnola.ch www.villacastagnola.com	René Nagy	68

Europe Middle East and Africa
HEAD OFFICE AND REGIONAL OFFICE
James House, Bridge Street, Leatherhead, Surrey KT22 7EP
T: 0044 (0) 1372 361873 F: 0044 (0) 1372 361874

Directory Requests: +44 (0) 1372 375116

The Americas
REGIONAL OFFICE
370 Lexington Avenue, Suite 1506, New York, NY 10017, USA
T: 001 212 953 2064 F: 001 212 953 0827

Directory Requests: +1 972 980 2555

Asia & Pacific
REGIONAL OFFICE
Suite 83 Chatswood Village, 47 Neridah Street, Chatswood, NSW 2067, Australia
T: 0061 (0) 2 9411 5532 F: 0061 (0) 2 9411 5534

Directory Requests: +61 (0) 2 9415 4577

www.slh.com